Black
Nationalism

Lucent Library of Black History

Black Nationalism

Lucent Library of Black History

Charles George

LUCENT BOOKS

A part of Gale, Cengage Learning

Detroit • New York • San Francisco • New Haven, Conn • Waterville, Maine • London

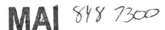

Acknowledgement
The author would like to express his gratitude to Lucile Davis for her invaluable assistance with this book. Without it, this project probably would not have been completed.

© 2009 Gale, Cengage Learning

LIBRARY OF CONGRESS CATALOGING-IN-PUBLICATION DATA

George, Charles, 1949–
  Black nationalism / by Charles George.
     p. cm. — (Lucent library of Black history)
  Includes bibliographical references and index.
  ISBN 978-1-4205-0083-7 (hardcover)
  1. Black nationalism—United States—History—19th century—Juvenile literature. 2. Black nationalism—United States—History—20th century—Juvenile literature. 3. Black nationalism—United States—Juvenile literature. 4. African Americans—Politics and government—19th century—Juvenile literature. 5. African Americans—Politics and government—20th century—Juvenile literature. I. Title.
  E185.61.G2858 2009
  320.54'60973—dc22
                                                          2009007229

Lucent Books
27500 Drake Rd.
Farmington Hills, MI 48331

ISBN-13: 978-1-4205-0083-7
ISBN-10: 1-4205-0083-X

Printed in the United States of America
 2 3 4 5 6 7 13 12 11 10

Printed by Bang Printing, Brainerd, MN, 2nd Ptg., 07/2010

Contents

Foreword

It has been more than 500 years since Africans were first brought to the New World in shackles, and over 140 years since slavery was formally abolished in the United States. Over 50 years have passed since the fallacy of "separate but equal" was obliterated in the American courts, and some 40 years since the watershed Civil Rights Act of 1965 guaranteed the rights and liberties of all Americans, especially those of color. Over time, these changes have become celebrated landmarks in American history. In the twenty-first century, African American men and women are politicians, judges, diplomats, professors, deans, doctors, artists, athletes, business owners, and home owners. For many, the scars of the past have melted away in the opportunities that have been found in contemporary society. Observers such as Peter N. Kirsanow, who sits on the U.S. Commission of Civil Rights, point to these accomplishments and conclude, "The growing black middle class may be viewed as proof that most of the civil rights battles have been won."

In spite of these legal victories, however, prejudice and inequality have persisted in American society. In 2003, African Americans comprised just 12 percent of the nation's population, yet accounted for 44 percent of its prison inmates and 24 percent of its poor. Racially motivated hate crimes continue to appear on the pages of major newspapers in many American cities. Furthermore, many African Americans still experience either overt or muted racism in their daily lives. A 1996 study undertaken by Professor Nancy Krieger of the Harvard School of Public Health, for example, found that 80 percent of the African American participants reported having experienced racial discrimination in one or more settings, including at work or school, applying for housing and medical care, from the police or in the courts, and on the street or in a public setting.

It is for these reasons that many believe the struggle for racial equality and justice is far from over. These episodes of discrimination threaten to shatter the illusion that America has completely overcome its racist past, causing many black Americans to become increasingly frustrated and confused. Scholar and writer Ellis Cose has described this splintered state in the following way: "I have done everything I was supposed to do. I have stayed out of trouble with the law, gone to the right schools, and worked myself nearly to death. What more do they want? Why in God's name won't they accept me as a full human being?" For Cose and others, the struggle for equality and justice has yet to be fully achieved.

In many subtle yet important ways the traumatic experiences of slavery and segregation continue to inform the way race is discussed and experienced in the twenty-first century. Indeed, it is possible that America will always grapple with the fallout from its distressing past. Ulric Haynes, dean of the Hofstra University School of Business has said, "Perhaps race will always matter, given the historical circumstances under which we came to this country." But studying this past and understanding how it contributes to present-day dialogues about race and history in America is a critical component of contemporary education. To this end, the Lucent Library of Black History offers a thorough look at the experiences that have shaped the black community and the American people as a whole. Annotated bibliographies provide readers with ideas for further research, while fully documented primary and secondary source quotations enhance the text. Each book in the series explores a different episode of black history; together they provide students with a wealth of information as well as launching points for further study and discussion.

Introduction

Black Nationalism in America

Black nationalism is a set of ideas, beliefs, and actions that promote racial pride for African Americans. It also advocates economic power, self-determination, and cultural separation of blacks from white society. Black nationalist thinking appeared in the United States to counter negative images of blacks created by the institution of slavery.

African slave labor was brought to America to raise the food to feed the colonies and grow trade crops, such as rice, indigo, and tobacco. This led to economic stability, which allowed the American colonies to declare independence from England. After independence, slave labor helped build the wealth of the fledgling United States, but slaves were not granted the rights of citizenship under the nation's Constitution.

Slavery created a moral dilemma in the American colonies that persisted into nationhood. Many people believed enslaving human beings was wrong, but the work done by black slaves left white people free to organize and to build wealth. This helped create a strong government that could stand alone without help from England or other European nations. This inner conflict—the immorality of slavery versus the practicality of having a cheap labor force—was not resolved. The issue of race continued to simmer, boiling to the surface during four periods in U.S. history—the late 1700s, the decades immediately preceding the American Civil War, the period between 1880 and the 1920s, and finally during the Civil Rights Movement of the 1950s and 1960s.

The first period, from 1790 to 1820, saw African slaves beginning to demand fair treatment. They realized that the promises of the U.S. Constitution—of life, liberty, and the pursuit of happiness—did not extend to black people. The second movement was in the 1840s and 1850s, when people, black and white, helped Africans escape slavery via the Underground Railroad, a loosely organized system designed to help slaves get to freedom in the North. This was also when black nationalist thinking developed, as free blacks met in convention to discuss the issue of inequality and how to fight against it.

A third period, from the 1880s to the 1920s, increased awareness of black nationalism when Jamaican-born Marcus Garvey formed the Universal Negro Improvement Association (UNIA). Garvey's organization worked to unite the black race into a separate nation. Colorful parades and large conventions by the UNIA brought public attention to the organization's demand for black self-determination and separation. Because of his efforts, some have called Marcus Garvey the father of black nationalism. The Civil Rights Movement of the 1960s, the fourth period and most widely known upsurge of black nationalist thinking and action, brought a highly visible demand for a change in the treatment of African Americans.

Black nationalist thinking is not limited to political and social arenas. It is also found in popular culture. Black nationalism lies at the center of hip-hop art and music that developed toward the end of the twentieth century. The hip-hop generation, born between 1964 and 1984, came of age in time to vote in the 2008 election. Through an organization known as the Hip-Hop Summit Action Network (HSAN) members of this generation are in position to step forward to demand social, economic, and political change. Their thinking and actions may determine the future of black nationalism.

Chapter One

What Is
Black Nationalism?

Nationalism, or pride in one's nation, is evident most often on national holidays, such as the Fourth of July, at political rallies, and during international sporting events, such as the Olympics or World Cup Soccer championships. Citizens wave their nation's flag, sing patriotic songs, or, in the case of political rallies, proudly display banners, hats, ribbons, posters, or flags featuring their favorite candidate or political party. All this is perfectly normal. In fact, it is highly encouraged, and those who do not participate in it often face criticism.

What, then, is black nationalism? Is it the patriotic feelings shared by citizens of black nations? No, in the nations of Africa and in other predominantly black nations like Haiti, nationalistic feelings are widespread and encouraged, but they are not referred to as black nationalism. They are Kenyan nationalism, Ugandan nationalism, Sudanese nationalism, Haitian nationalism, and so forth. In other words, they are based upon each particular country's identity, not upon racial identity.

In the United States, however, black nationalism is a widely accepted term that describes a particular social, political, cultural, and economic concept—the unity and pride of black people, and in some cases, a desire to separate completely from white society. Why, then, is such a term used here in the United States, but not in the rest of the world? The answer lies in the historic relationship between whites and blacks.

Roots of Racial Conflict in the United States

Tension between whites and blacks in the United States is not new. It began long before the nation was founded. African slaves were transported against their will to North America beginning as early as the 1600s, and their labor helped create the strong economy that enabled North American colonies to declare independence from England.

The first slaves were brought to America in 1619.

The North American colonies were largely established through the aid of the British government. At first the colonies depended on England for supplies and military protection. The British government taxed the colonies for these services. African slave labor changed the colonies' dependence on the English. The first slaves arrived in North America in 1619. The African slave trade grew slowly until 1672, when the English established the Royal African Company. The company monopolized the Triangle Trade that sent trade goods to Africa in exchange for slaves, who were transported to America and exchanged for goods that were then shipped to England.

Land in North America was plentiful, and African slaves provided the work force to farm the land. Slaves worked from sunup to sundown to produce cash crops such as rice, indigo, and tobacco. These crops were grown in large quantities and exported to other countries. The wealth these commercial crops produced allowed the colonies to become economically independent. Economic independence allowed the colonists to establish

Triangle Slave Trade

Slavery is as old as human civilization. African slaves labored in most of the major empires of the world, including ancient Egypt, Rome, and the Ottoman Empire. Enslaved Africans were transported to Europe after the bubonic plague killed much of the continent's work force in 1380. When Europeans colonized the Americas, they brought their slaves with them. Soon, merchants dealing in slaves put the American continents on their trade routes.

Goods from Europe went to Africa and were traded for slaves. Slaves were shipped to the Americas, and profits from the sale of those slaves bought American raw materials, such as cotton, sugar, tobacco, and molasses. These raw materials were shipped to Europe to be exchanged for manufactured goods that would then be sent on to Africa for more slaves. This Triangle Trade expanded the world economy of the eighteenth and early nineteenth centuries and created the wealth that funded the Industrial Revolution.

their own military and to build ships to conduct trade. Colonists soon came to resent having to pay taxes for services they did not need. The large slave labor force kept working. The slaves produced the commercial crops, as well as food crops, while the colonies' military fought the war for independence from England.

When the United States of America broke from England, our Declaration of Independence stated the belief that "all men are created equal, that they are endowed by their Creator with certain unalienable Rights, that among these are Life, Liberty and the pursuit of Happiness." The equality that our founding fathers envisioned, however, did not extend to African slaves. In fact, any mention by delegates to the Continental Congress of abolishing slavery threatened to block approval of the declaration. Many of the largest slave holders were delegates to the congress from Southern states. Their personal wealth and that of their states depended on slave labor. Many of the Northern delegates were also reluctant to free the slaves. Some Northerners were afraid that freed blacks would seek bloody revenge on those who enslaved them or profited from their labor. These same reasons kept the abolition of slavery out of the U.S. Constitution.

The Constitution, ratified in 1788, mentioned slavery, but in no way sought to abolish it. Instead, it codified—or wrote into law—the practice, going so far as to establish that each slave was to be counted as three-fifths of a person for the purposes of taxation and representation. As slaves, Africans had no rights, no status, and no place in American society. The American Civil Liberties Union (ACLU) once noted:

> [The] Constitution protected slavery and legalized racial subordination. Instead of constitutional rights, slaves were governed by "slave codes" that controlled every aspect of their lives. They had no access to the rule of law; they could not go to court, make contracts, or own any property. They could be shipped, branded, imprisoned without trial, and hanged.[1]

After President Abraham Lincoln issued the Emancipation Proclamation in 1863, declaring slaves in the Confederacy free, 1865 brought the end of the Civil War and ratification of the Thirteenth Amendment, which officially abolished slavery. Next, the restored Union added the Fourteenth and Fifteenth Amendments to the U.S.

A group of slaves gathers to await word of the Emancipation Proclamation that will give them their freedom.

Constitution (1868 and 1870, respectively), providing equal protection under the law for former slaves and guaranteeing their right to vote.

White Southerners, however, were not ready to grant rights to a race they considered less than human. Black slavery had always been a troubling issue for whites. One human enslaving another seemed immoral. Over time, however, white slave owners developed a set of racial theories that seemed to prove that blacks were subhuman. Under these theories, if blacks were subhuman, they could not (and should not) be granted human rights.

Southern states passed Jim Crow laws, named for a character in a pre–Civil War minstrel song, which made it difficult, if not impossible, for African Americans to vote, own land, or move freely in public. Jim Crow was not just a set of legal measures. It became a national mind-set, institutionalizing discrimination and prejudice against African Americans. Until the Civil Rights Movement of the mid-twentieth century, these laws effectively prohibited interracial marriage, required separate public accommodations, and made it illegal for whites to serve, teach, medically treat, or do business with blacks. In essence, it all but guaranteed second-class citizenship to African Americans in most parts of the country.

Jim Crow laws in the Southern states legalized the segregation of races. Here, a black family must wait for their train in a separate waiting room than white people.

The Rise of Black Nationalism

Black nationalism developed in the United States to counter the effects of slavery and the later Jim Crow thinking that denied African Americans an equal place in a country that was founded on the principles of freedom and equal justice under the law. No one group of people met at a particular place or on a specific date to define black nationalism. It has been defined and redefined as African Americans have responded to the social and political needs and circumstances of various periods in U.S. history.

An agreement on the definition of black nationalism is hard to find. The beliefs of black nationalist thinking, however, have always included racial pride, self-determination, economic power, and some form of separation from white society. Black nationalist thinking developed in the United States because of a need among those of African descent to band together to fight the racial prejudice created by the institution of slavery in America.

Chapter Two

Beginnings of Black Nationalism

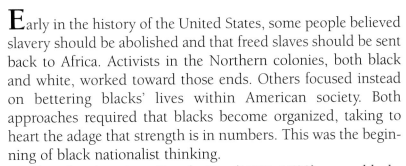

Early in the history of the United States, some people believed slavery should be abolished and that freed slaves should be sent back to Africa. Activists in the Northern colonies, both black and white, worked toward those ends. Others focused instead on bettering blacks' lives within American society. Both approaches required that blacks become organized, taking to heart the adage that strength is in numbers. This was the beginning of black nationalist thinking.

After the American Revolution (1775–1783) some blacks were able to gain their freedom, but they found that freedom did not necessarily bring independence. Many felt the solution to this problem required African Americans to break away from white control, since whites had controlled virtually every aspect of the slaves' lives. Blacks in the North began the separation process by founding independent religious and social organizations. Black nationalism developed in these places under the leadership of educated African Americans, who stepped forward and risked every bit as much as the country's white founders had risked when breaking away from the British Empire.

Black Churches

Black churches existed in the American colonies prior to the Revolution. First to appear were Negro Baptist churches, established in Virginia and Georgia in the early 1770s. However, these churches were part of the white-controlled Baptist denomination, despite each congregation being under the leadership of black pastors. The first truly autonomous black church in the United States was the African Methodist Episcopal Church, or AME, and its founder was Richard Allen.

Allen, a former slave, was a preacher and a member of the white-controlled St. George's Methodist Episcopal Church in Philadelphia, Pennsylvania. He recognized the need for an organization that would bring blacks together to address social problems in the community. In particular, Allen was critical of discrimination he saw among his congregation. Blacks could attend St. George's, but were required to sit or stand at the back of the sanctuary. A disagreement over this practice eventually led to a walkout by black members of St. George's congregation.

One of the first autonomous black churches was the Mother Bethel African Methodist Episcopal Church in Philadelphia, Pennsylvania.

After the walkout, Allen and fellow member Absalom Jones established a benevolent society called the Free African Society (FAS) in 1786. A benevolent society is a community service organization. FAS kept black churchgoers in touch with each other and provided the organization and money they needed to build their own church. Allen purchased land and paid to have an old blacksmith shop moved to the site as a temporary meeting place until a permanent structure could be built. Once finished, Bethel African Methodist Episcopal Church, later nicknamed Mother Bethel, was dedicated in 1794.

Two years later a white member of St. George's somehow tricked Allen into signing the property back over to the Methodist Episcopal Church. For several years Allen and his congregation had to fight against interference from the white denomination in the running of their church. Then, in 1815 the Methodist Episcopalians put Bethel up for auction, and Allen bought back his own church. Despite this, deacons and officers of St. George's still tried to direct the Bethel congregation until a court case in 1816 finally freed Bethel from the control of the Methodist Episcopal denomination.

After Bethel won its freedom, Allen learned that other black congregations had experienced the same kind of discrimination. In describing the founding of Bethel, Allen wrote, "Our colored friends in Baltimore were treated in a similar manner by the white preachers and trustees. . . . Many of the colored people in other places were in a situation nearly like those of Philadelphia and Baltimore, which induced us, in April 1816, to call a general meeting."[2]

The meeting of independent black churches established a new denomination. It became known as the African Methodist Episcopal Church (AME). Allen was elected its first bishop, and Bethel was acknowledged as the "Mother Church" of the denomination. Nearly a century later, black educator and activist W.E.B. Du Bois called Mother Bethel "the vastest and most remarkable product of American Negro civilization."[3]

Bethel Church became a place where blacks could gather, find help, and talk about the social and political challenges they faced. Black nationalist beliefs developed within the caring community created by Bishop Allen in and around Bethel Church. In addi-

The Underground Railroad

"Underground Railroad" was a term applied to a loosely organized system that helped fugitive slaves to escape Southern slavery for safety in Canada or to free states in the northern United States. There were no actual trains or tracks involved. The term first appeared in print in 1840. Other railroad terms were used to describe the process of moving slaves out of the South. Escaping slaves were called "passengers." Safe houses, where slaves were allowed to stay overnight, were known as "stations." Those who guided slaves along their path to freedom were called "conductors."

The Underground Railroad was not the result of a large organization. Help came voluntarily and on the spur of the moment from people sympathetic to the plight of runaway slaves. White sympathizers were not the only ones involved. Free blacks in the North and South also participated. Black slaves helped fugitives escape the plantations. The fugitive slaves played a major part in their own escape. They had to make most of the trip out of the South alone before they could find "conductors" and "stations" on the Underground Railroad.

Slaves escaping to freedom via the Underground Railroad.

tion to providing a place where blacks felt comfortable openly discussing their collective and individual situations, it also provided a degree of separation from white society.

Bethel established and supported a children's day school and an adult night school in the church building. Before and during the American Civil War, the basement of the building also became a stop for the Underground Railroad, the secret network of people and places that helped runaway slaves make their way to freedom.

Benevolent Societies

Other benevolent societies, similar to Allen's FAS, were established in other cities and states. Many, like FAS, were founded by African Americans forced out of white church congregations. These societies provided some services that were usually performed by churches, such as funerals and burials. They also offered financial aid in case of sickness or death.

Black benevolent societies also helped people economically. In the nineteenth century they provided financial and organizational help to black-owned banks and insurance companies. These societies operated much like modern chambers of commerce by providing a place for black businessmen to meet, form partnerships, and share advice. African Americans were able to communicate within local benevolent societies and with societies in other cities.

Separation Through Colonization

Churches and benevolent societies worked to create a better life for blacks within the United States. Some, however, believed blacks could never achieve equality in the United States. They thought those of African descent would never achieve self-determination until they returned to their home continent of Africa.

Paul Cuffe (1759–1817) was a former slave who became a prosperous merchant in Massachusetts. Born to a Native American mother and African American father, he had purchased his own freedom and eventually established his own shipping company. Cuffe was a devout Quaker and worked to improve the conditions of African Americans and to abolish slavery. Through his contacts with English Quakers, he heard of the Sierra Leone

Colony in West Africa. The British had established the colony to resettle freed slaves.

After first traveling there to investigate, he organized a small group of American blacks willing to relocate to Africa. In 1815 Cuffe financed a voyage for thirty-eight blacks to settle in Sierra Leone, where he helped them establish new homes. Encouraged by his success, he returned to the United States to start another group. Before he could continue his plan, however, his health failed.

At about the same time, another organization was established, this one, oddly enough, having the support of some Southern slave owners. The American Colonization Society (ACS), founded in 1816, worked to help free blacks emigrate to Africa. A white New Jersey Presbyterian minister, Robert Finley, originally formed the group as a charitable mission. He believed emigration would benefit American blacks and Africans alike by spreading Christianity and ending slavery.

However, officers and members of ACS were white, and their motives varied. Some were genuinely concerned for free blacks. Others, notably Southern slave owners, wanted to continue slavery in the United States but wanted to rid the country of free blacks. They did not believe America could be a biracial society, with blacks and whites living and working together.

The ACS worked with the U.S. government to establish the West African colony of Liberia in 1821, eventually settling more than fifteen thousand freed slaves there. The ACS sought the support of American blacks, but many were skeptical of its white membership and of its motives. Many blacks, the vast majority of whom had been born in the United States, also feared the possibility of forced deportation.

A group of "free people of color," as they called themselves, met in Richmond, Virginia, in 1817 to consider the colonization question. They issued the following carefully worded response: "We prefer being colonized in the most remote corner of the land of our nativity, to being exiled to a foreign country."[4] Despite this feeling, which was shared by many freed blacks, white members of organizations like the ACS resisted the idea of settling African Americans in North America, fearing they would ally themselves with American Indian tribes or neighboring foreign powers during times of war.

Some blacks, though suspicious of the ACS but still interested in returning to Africa, formed the African Civilization Society in the mid-1800s. This organization supposedly promoted "the civilization and Christianization of Africa and of the descendants of African ancestors."[5] Frederick Douglass (1818–1895) and other black leaders, however, had doubts about the African Civilization

Frederick Douglass

Frederick Douglass was born Frederick Bailey, a slave of Thomas Auld, a Maryland plantation owner. At age eight, he was sent to Baltimore to work as a houseboy for Auld's brother Hugh. There, Hugh's wife taught Frederick how to read. The boy began to read abolitionist texts and spent time with lay preachers who talked of freedom. This experience led him to form a sense of his own manhood. He escaped to New York where he changed his name to Douglass and became a leading abolitionist, a popular speaker, and a successful newspaper publisher. After the Civil War, Douglas prospered. He served as marshal of Washington, D.C., as the city's recorder of deeds, and as consul general to Haiti from 1889 to 1891.

Douglass opposed both the American Colonization Society and the African Civilization Society. He believed in self-determination. He said, "If colored men are convinced that they can better their condition by going to Africa . . . we shall respect them if they will go. . . . But widely different is the case, when men combine in societies . . . to collect money and call upon us to help them travel from continent to continent."

Quoted in Wilson Jeremiah Moses, ed., *Classical Black Nationalism: From the American Revolution to Marcus Garvey*. New York: New York University Press, 1996, p. 140.

Frederick Douglass.

Society, believing it was a front for the white-run American Colonization Society.

National Black Conventions

As African American groups banded together for aid and support—through black churches, benevolent societies, or African colonization organizations—another idea arose that combined the benefits of all three and provided a forum for free and open discussion of options: a national black convention. The first to suggest such a gathering, in September 1830, was a free black man from Baltimore, Maryland—Hezekiah Grice. He corresponded with Richard Allen, and the first convention took place at Allen's Bethel Church in Philadelphia.

Other conventions followed annually from 1830 to 1860 and led to a more centralized and organized black nationalism. Political and social issues of importance to African Americans were discussed and "statements of purpose" written and approved. The second convention, for example, resolved to raise money for the black refugees in Canada, but also discussed and approved black temperance societies, a boycott of slave-made products, and a call to petition for the abolition of slavery. Later conventions continued to support petitions to the government for African American rights and discussions on emigration. Delegates also approved resolutions to raise money to establish black vocational schools, benevolent societies, and support for black-owned enterprises.

In welcoming delegates to the fourth national convention, held in 1834, convention chairman William Hamilton stated why he felt these meetings were necessary: "Under present circumstances it is highly necessary the free people of colour should combine and closely attend to their own particular interests . . . to take into consideration what are the best means to promote their elevation, and . . . to pursue those means with . . . zeal until their end is obtained."[6]

During this time, many African American leaders saw emigration as the answer to independence and equality for Negroes. Emigration became a major topic at black conventions. Delegates at the first convention decided in favor of emigration to Canada. A colony of black people had already been established there. Subsequent conventions continued discussing emigration, but also considered other issues.

After 1835 most conventions were on a state-by-state basis rather than nationwide. The issue of emigration, however, remained a major focus of these conventions. The idea of establishing a black nation became a major point in black nationalist thinking. This geographic separatist idea usually advocated a black nation in Africa, but other locations were considered, and additional colonies of blacks settled in Canada, Jamaica, and Haiti. Black separatists believed only relocation away from the United States would allow them to escape the control of white society.

Some African American leaders disagreed, believing the United States offered the best chance for freedom and opportunity. They saw integration into the United States' social and political system as the best way for blacks to be accepted as equals. Black integrationists sought to reform the U.S. legal system and advance black economic power to gain independence and respect for their race. One of the key figures in this debate was Booker T. Washington (1856–1915), founder and head of the Tuskegee Institute. He believed education was the key to African Americans' goals of independence from whites.

The debate between separatists and integrationists often appeared in print. David Walker (1785–1830), a black author of the early nineteenth century, supported abolishing slavery and working for black equality on American soil. Walker's most

Booker T. Washington was a leader of the integrationists, those who believed black people could make better lives for themselves by staying in America and integrating with white society.

famous work was a pamphlet titled *Appeal in Four Articles*, published in 1829. In it he urged slaves to rise up against their masters and free themselves. He advised slaves to separate themselves from the white man's control, but did not call for an exodus to Africa or elsewhere. "America is more our country than it is the whites," he stated. "We have enriched it with our blood and tears. The greatest riches in all America have arisen from our blood and tears."[7]

The Black Press and the Debate over Emigration

The debate over whether to stay in the United States or start a new black nation somewhere else became a major topic for the black press. About forty black-owned and black-edited newspapers were published in the United States before the Civil War. These helped spread black nationalist ideas. The papers printed articles that promoted racial pride, encouraged education for blacks, and debated the issues important to the black community. The debate over emigration, though, found space in almost every issue.

The first black newspaper, *Freedom's Journal*, debated the issue rather intensely. *Freedom's Journal* began publication on March 16, 1827, in New York City. Its articles concentrated on the emigration debate, which eventually led to the paper's demise when its founding editors, Samuel E. Cornish and John B. Russwurm, parted ways over the issue in 1829. Russwurm favored emigration, so he moved to Africa, where he published a newspaper

Masthead of the first issue of the first black newspaper, *Freedom's Journal*.

FREEDOM'S JOURNAL

" *RIGHTEOUSNESS EXALTETH A NATION.* "

NEW-YORK, FRIDAY, MARCH 16, 1827.

works of trivial importance, we shall consider it a part of our duty to recommend to our young readers, such authors as will not only enlarge their stock of useful knowledge, but such as will also serve to stimulate them to higher at- narrative which they have published; the establishment of the republic of Hayti after year sanguinary warfare ; its subsequent pr in all the arts of civilization ; and vancement of liberal ideas in Sou' called the *Liberia Herald*. Cornish stayed in the United States and started his own paper, *The Rights of All*.

Cornish and Russwurm were not the only publishing partners to disagree. Frederick Douglass and his partner, Martin R. Delany (1812–1885), also held opposite opinions. Frederick Douglass's *North Star* was the most influential black newspaper in the nation. His paper began publication in 1847. It made Douglass a leading voice for immediate abolition of slavery by any means.

Douglass worked for abolition, but his black nationalist thinking supported reforming the country's institutions. He did not believe emigration would provide blacks with the opportunities they could achieve in the United States. "Certainly there is no place on the globe where the colored man can speak to a larger audience, either by precept or by example, than in the United States."[8]

Although Douglass stood against emigration, Delany, his publishing partner at the *North Star*, was a separatist, intent on creating a new black nation in Africa. Delany and Douglass had met at an antislavery rally in 1847 in Pittsburgh. Out of this meeting came the idea for the newspaper, and Delany's views in favor of emigration appeared in the *North Star* along with Douglass's view opposing it.

Martin Delany and Emigration

Delany's belief in the rightness of African colonization came from his own life experiences. His mother's parents were born in Africa. His attempts to advance within the United States had little success. He studied medicine and interned with a number of practicing physicians for more than fifteen years. However, when Delany applied for medical school at Harvard University in 1850, with seventeen letters of support from Northern doctors, a protest from a group of white students succeeded in having Delany and two other black students dismissed.

His experience at Harvard convinced Delany that no reasonable argument could persuade whites to allow blacks an equal place in society. "[I] would as willingly live among white as black, if I had an equal possession and enjoyment of privileges; but shall never be reconciled to live among them, subservient to their will—existing by mere sufferances, as we, the colored people, do in this country."[9]

Separatist Martin Delany believed that American blacks should create a new black nation in Africa.

Passage of the Fugitive Slave Act of 1850 made it possible to put any black, free or slave from the North or South, on trial as a fugitive. It put every free black at risk for being returned to slavery. This confirmed Delany's belief that the only self-respecting response for blacks was to leave the United States. Four years later, in 1854, he helped organize the Negro Emigration Convention that met in Cleveland, Ohio. At the convention, he advanced the idea of colonizing Africa.

Most speakers and delegates at the convention favored emigration, but a major resolution in the convention's "Declaration of Sentiments" overshadowed the separatist argument. They stated: "That, as men and equals, we demand every political right, privilege and position to which the whites are eligible in the United States, and we will either attain to these, or accept of nothing."[10] Despite earlier efforts to organize black churches and benevolent societies, this resolution is often cited as the foundation of black nationalist thinking.

After the convention Delany traveled to Liberia to make the contacts necessary to allow American blacks to start moving to Africa. He signed treaties with eight chiefs to allow settlement on tribal lands, but war, both in Africa and in America, brought a halt to Delany's emigration plans. Tribal wars in Africa made his treaties useless, and by the time he returned to the United States, the American Civil War had begun. Delany decided to stay in the United States and work to free the slaves.

Fugitive Slave Act of 1850

The Fugitive Slave Act of 1850, passed by the United States Congress, was part of a compromise between Northern and Southern legislators. California was allowed to enter the Union as a free state in exchange for harsher treatment of suspected runaway slaves in the North.

The Fugitive Slave Act allowed federal commissioners to try any free or slave black without a jury. In fact, the law paid commissioners a double fee if the suspect were declared a fugitive slave. No testimony for the accused was allowed. This effectively made every free black a potential slave.

Though black nationalists of the nineteenth century debated how to achieve racial pride and separation from white society, one point stood out: African American self-reliance was the key. As Delany put it, "Our elevation must be the result of self-efforts, and work of our own hands. These are the proper and only means of elevating ourselves and attaining equality in this country or any other."[11]

Chapter Three

From Reconstruction to the Civil Rights Movement

The American Civil War (1861–1865) was supposed to have been fought to solve the nation's slavery problem (among others), and it appeared to have succeeded. However, white prejudice against freed slaves in the South created another, more complex problem—how to integrate a large number of former slaves into U.S. politics and culture. Despite having gained their freedom, blacks found it almost impossible to be treated equally, much less to take their rightful place in American society and politics.

During Reconstruction (the period following the Civil War, from 1865 to 1877), African Americans were able to exercise their civil rights. For the first time, blacks living in the South could own property and hold elective office. In less than twenty years, however, white Southerners regained political and economic control by passing Jim Crow laws, effectively denying civil and voting rights for African Americans and ensuring segregation between the races. By 1900, most states had some form of legal segregation. Blacks may not have been slaves any more, but they certainly were less than equal under the law. As a result of this widespread practice in the South, thousands of newly freed blacks made their way north.

The Great Migration

In response to Jim Crow laws, African Americans left the South and moved to northern cities, forever changing the demographics of the nation. Black migration from Southern to Northern states lasted through the 1960s. In the last decade of the 1800s, 90 percent of the nation's blacks lived in the South. By the 1960s about 30 percent had moved north.

This demographic shift created increased tension between the races. Southern blacks moved northward in the hope of finding safer living conditions. The reality was quite different. As more and more blacks moved to large Northern cities, the races collided, causing friction. Northern whites resented the intrusion, and blacks again found themselves threatened by violence aimed at keeping them subservient.

No constitutional amendment—no civil law—could suddenly elevate blacks in the eyes of the white community. Old ideas formed during the slavery years—that the Negro race was childlike in its thinking, lazy, and less than fully human—continued to color white opinions. Whites believed black people incapable of becoming part of a civilized society.

Jim Crow was not just a set of legal measures. It was a mindset that allowed whites to treat blacks as second-class citizens. And the Jim Crow mind-set existed in the North as well as in the South. Black leaders rose to address the problem, but once again the debate developed over how to counter the effects of Jim Crow thinking. Key to that debate were two individuals—Booker T. Washington and W.E.B. Du Bois. Their debate marked the beginning of the third period of intense black nationalism.

The Washington-Du Bois Debate

Washington (1856–1915), black educator and founder of the Tuskegee Institute in Alabama, thought education and economic

W.E.B. Du Bois

William Edward Burghardt Du Bois grew up in Massachusetts. His mother was a domestic worker. His father, a barber, left the family while William was very young.

Du Bois attended school but lost his mother before he finished his schooling. He went to work in a mill but still managed to be the first African American to graduate from his high school. He continued his education at Fisk University and went on to graduate in 1895 from Harvard University with a PhD in history.

Du Bois's life had changed when he attended Fisk University in Nashville, Tennessee. Growing up in Massachusetts, he had had very little contact with other African Americans. At Fisk, he came to know the African American culture and to experience racism. His experiences in Nashville helped shape his ideas on race relations.

Those ideas would become public with the publication in 1903 of *The Souls of Black Folk*, a powerful collection of essays about being black in the United States. His book was so successful and so influential, it propelled Du Bois into a leadership position in the black community. Black educator William H. Ferris explained it this way in 1913:

"Du Bois is one of the few men in history who was hurled on the throne of leadership by the dynamic force of the written word. He is one of the few writers who leaped to the front as a leader and became the head of a popular movement through impressing his personality upon men by means of a book."

Quoted in Henry Louis Gates Jr., introduction to *The Souls of Black Folk*, by W.E.B. Du Bois. New York: Bantam Classic Edition, 1989, p. viii.

W.E.B. Du Bois.

self-reliance would bring equality and independence to former slaves. Du Bois (1868–1963), one of the founders of the National Association for the Advancement of Colored People (NAACP), called for African Americans to take immediate social and political action to demand their rights under the U.S. Constitution.

This introduced a new debate into black nationalist thought. Both Washington and Du Bois were integrationists, and both advocated working within the United States sociopolitical system. Washington's black nationalism, however, was expressed in economic terms, while Du Bois's nationalism advocated direct political action.

The violence against African Americans that erupted in the South during Reconstruction bothered Washington. He sought a solution. A lifelong resident of the South, he knew whites would not and could not share political power with blacks. Firm in his belief that money brought power, Washington spoke to the need for African Americans to acquire an education and vocational skills in order to become economically independent. Economic power would, he believed, enable African Americans to gain the political power necessary to achieve their civil rights.

Washington developed the Tuskegee Institute based on this idea. Tuskegee Institute was founded by Lewis Adams, a former slave, and George W. Campbell, a former slave owner. After the slaves were freed, both men worried that without education the former slaves would not be able to support themselves. They founded Tuskegee to address this concern.

Neither man had experience with educational institutions, so they needed someone with experience to be head of the school. A letter to Hampton Institute in Virginia asking for a recommendation brought Washington's name to their attention. Washington had been working at the Hampton Institute as a teacher. At the age of twenty-five, Washington accepted the position of head of the Tuskegee Institute. The school opened on July 4, 1881. A plantation was purchased and buildings constructed by students who earned all or part of the expenses. The school provided training for teachers, farmers, and trades such as metalworking, building, and manufacturing.

Asked to give a speech at the 1895 Cotton States Exposition in Atlanta, Georgia, Washington was worried. He could promote his

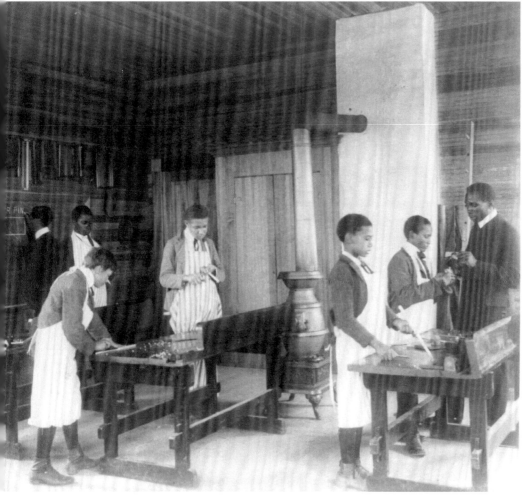

Students at a workshop at the Tuskegee Institute.

idea of vocational training for African Americans, but any hint of protest against racism would turn the predominantly white audience against him. After all, he had relied on white support to keep the Tuskegee Institute funded. A negative reaction to his speech could damage his reputation and the success of Tuskegee. He chose his words carefully, offering constructive criticism to his own race:

> Our greatest danger is that in the great leap from slavery to freedom, we may overlook the fact that the masses of us

are to live by the productions of our hands, and fail to keep in our mind that we shall prosper in the proportion as we learn to dignify and glorify common labor and put our brains and skill into the common occupations of life. . . . No race can prosper till it learns that there is as much dignity in tilling a field as in writing a poem. It is at the bottom of life we should begin and not the top.[12]

He closed his "Atlanta Compromise" speech with the analogy that blacks and whites could be like fingers on a hand—separated socially, but united for progress.

Washington's audience stood and cheered. The white press reported the speech across the nation, and politicians, former

Booker T. Washington and the Tuskegee Institute

Born a slave in Virginia, Booker T. Washington had a curiosity that drove him to obtain an education. He worked in a salt mine at night and attended school during the day. Upon graduation, he went on to advanced studies at Hampton Normal and Agricultural Institute in Norfolk, Virginia. There, he worked as the school's janitor to pay his tuition. Hampton was an industrial school for African Americans and American Indians. While at Hampton, Washington observed how Samuel C. Armstrong, the institute's president, ran the school and how he won the admiration of its students and the support of the white community.

When Washington completed his studies at Hampton in 1875, he was asked to teach there, and when the Alabama legislature contacted Armstrong for the name of a teacher who could found another school for blacks at Tuskegee, Alabama, he recommended Washington. In 1881 Washington founded the Normal School for Colored Teachers, later called the Tuskegee Institute. The school provided teacher education and vocational education for African Americans. Beginning with only one small shanty and a church, Washington built the school into what is today Tuskegee University, with over 150 buildings on 5,000 acres (2,024ha). Tuskegee was founded on the idea that the black race could (and would) achieve advancement in American society through acquiring practical knowledge and using that knowledge to earn a living.

abolitionists, business tycoons, leaders of both races, and President Grover Cleveland contacted Washington to congratulate him. Many people in the country felt Washington's speech had settled the race question once and for all.

Washington's mainstream black nationalist views appealed to many people in both races. But there were those in the black community who thought Washington was an appeaser, an accommodator—that he had caused irreparable harm to the cause of black equality. They felt that his carefully worded speech had bowed too low to white society and that he had all but admitted the superiority of whites.

Demand for Action

Du Bois's reputation and livelihood did not depend upon whites. As the first African American to earn a PhD from Harvard and as the author of a widely read and powerful collection of essays on the black experience in the United States, *The Souls of Black Folk*, published in 1903, he could speak directly and forcefully about his black nationalist views. He did not believe African Americans could gain pride in their race as long as they were kept out of the established society of the United States.

Ten years after Washington's speech in Atlanta, Georgia, Du Bois and a group of twenty-seven people gathered in the home of a member of the Michigan Street Baptist Church in Buffalo, New York. Resolutions passed at that meeting led to the founding of the Niagara movement, which then led to the founding of the National Association for the Advancement of Colored People (NAACP).

The Niagara movement, organized at Niagara Falls, argued against Washington's so-called "answer to the race question." For the African American men who met at the Falls, the black nationalist goal of racial pride could never be achieved without gaining the civil rights guaranteed to all citizens of the United States. The group published their demands in a statement written by Du Bois: "We will not be satisfied to take one jot or tittle less than our full manhood rights. We claim for ourselves every single right that belongs to a freeborn American, political, civil and social; and until we get these rights we will never cease to protest and assail the ears of America. . . . We are men; we will be treated as men. . . . And we shall win."[13]

The original leaders of the Niagara movement, posing in front of the
Niagara waterfalls in 1905. W.E.B. Du Bois is seated second from the
right in the center row.

Du Bois and the NAACP

Despite its worthy intention to achieve racial equality, the Niagara movement was unable to overcome a lack of funds and a lack of broad-based support. In 1908 Du Bois invited a white female social worker to join the group. Soon, other interested whites joined. On the one-hundredth anniversary of Abraham Lincoln's birth, February 12, 1909, Du Bois, along with blacks and whites in the Niagara movement, formed the National Association for the Advancement of Colored People (NAACP). The Niagara movement disbanded soon afterward.

The NAACP provided a strong organization of people of both races who worked together to oppose discrimination in laws and social practices. This mainstream organization appealed to Americans of both races by advocating an orderly process that promoted nonviolent protest and civil rights challenges within the American legal system.

The agenda of the NAACP reflected Du Bois's black nationalist feelings that blacks could best succeed within the United States, not by leaving it. However, despite a rapidly expanding membership, a widely distributed and much-read monthly magazine called *The Crisis*, and chapters in several major cities, the NAACP could never seem to attract the enthusiastic crowds necessary to ignite the country into action. Another black leader was on the way, though, who would do just that—an immigrant from Jamaica by the name of Marcus Garvey.

Cover of the first issue of *The Crisis*, the official publication of the NAACP.

Garveyism, a Movement with Style

Marcus Mosiah Garvey (1887–1940) was born in Jamaica in 1887. He attended school where white and black children learned and played together. Young Garvey was unaware of any distinction between the races until he reached his teens, when he learned his former schoolmates had been warned to stay away from him because of his race. He later said he never felt inferior to his white classmates. In fact, he wrote in an autobiographical article for the magazine *Current History* in 1923, that they had actually looked up to him.

He quit school at fourteen to become a printer's apprentice. At eighteen he managed a large print shop. Despite his position in management, Garvey helped organize a printers union. Owners of the print shop promised him big rewards if he would stop, but he refused and was fired and blackballed as a printer.

Unable to find work in Jamaica, he worked his way through countries in South America and Europe. No matter where he went, he later wrote, he "saw the injustice done to my race because it was black, and I became dissatisfied on that account."[14] While in London, Garvey read Booker T. Washington's autobiography *Up From Slavery*. Reading of the condition of black people in America led him to make a decision about his future, that he was destined to be a leader of his race:

> I read *Up From Slavery* . . . and then my doom—if I may so call it—of being a race leader dawned upon me in London after I had traveled through almost half of Europe. I asked, "Where is the black man's Government?" "Where is his King and Kingdom?" "Where is his President, his country, and his ambassador, his army, his navy, his men of big affairs?" I could not find them, and then I decided, "I will help to make them."[15]

Garvey returned to Jamaica in 1914 and founded the Universal Negro Improvement Association (UNIA). Organized as a fraternal and philanthropic group, the UNIA concentrated on lifting blacks out of their worldwide place as an inferior race, to "unite the black race through race pride, education, the redemption of Africa and economic development."[16] In 1917 he traveled to the United States to establish chapters here.

Garvey made his way to Harlem in New York City, and began to speak of the ill treatment blacks received and the advantages of the UNIA. He found a receptive audience. Many in his audience were black soldiers recently returned from fighting in Europe in World War I (1914–1918). The contrast between the liberty that black soldiers experienced in Europe and the restrictions imposed upon them in the United States was dramatic. They listened, but the newly formed black middle class and black leaders did not.

Garvey, however, did not give up. Two years later he used a near-tragic assault on his life by an insane man to his advantage. The press called it an assassination attempt, and the story was covered extensively. Almost immediately, Garvey became the symbol of, and the solution for, all the unhappiness that African Americans, and particularly those in the working class, had experienced.

Garvey succeeded where Washington and Du Bois had largely failed—in successfully reaching black working men and women. These people, with little education and low-paying jobs, needed someone they understood, someone like them. Garvey fit that profile, and he knew how to work a crowd. UNIA membership increased, and Garvey went on a thirty-eight state tour. When he returned to Harlem, he hired a hall, started publishing a newspaper, the *Negro World*, and began to raise money to support his unique brand of black nationalism.

Garvey's black nationalist ideas became known as Garveyism. He borrowed money, bought a building, and named it Liberty Hall. There, he preached his black nationalist views of racial pride and self-help, while raising more money. He used that money to buy the first ship for a black-owned merchant marine company he called the Black Star Line. The launching of the first ship drew thousands of people, and Garvey's speech was met with thunderous applause. "Up, you mighty race," he thundered. "You can accomplish what you will."[17] The statement became the rallying cry of Garveyism.

Garvey in Harlem

By 1923 crowds of African Americans drawn to Garveyism traveled to Harlem, to Liberty Hall. They came from all over the United States and from islands in the Caribbean. Membership in his UNIA swelled to over 2 million worldwide. One writer, Roi Ottley, witnessed firsthand this phenomenon, and wrote:

> Garvey's movement had gathered terrific momentum, even to a detail like the manufacture of black baby dolls for children. Negroes swept into Harlem, carried on a tidal wave of race consciousness. The cotton-picker of the South, bending over his basket, the poor ignorant worker of the Delta, crushed beneath a load of prejudice, the domestic of the city, trudging wearily to white folks' kitchens, and even the peasant of the Caribbean islands, dispossessed from the land, lifted his head and cried, "Let's go to Harlem and follow this Black Moses!"[18]

Garvey spoke about the redemption of Africa. His back-to-Africa movement, like Martin R. Delany's earlier colonization efforts, advocated a geographically separate black nation. He urged blacks the world over to consider themselves part of a black nation, and to work aggressively to build institutions and businesses that would support the well-being of all blacks.

Garvey depended on pomp and ceremony to keep his movement in the news. He formed a black social order and handed out titles to his friends and associates. He named himself provisional president-general of Africa and began wearing a military-style uniform, complete with a plumed hat. According to one writer, Garvey "felt that the logic of an all-black world demanded a *Black God*. So his official historians and theologians studied Biblical writings, reconstructed the nativity of Jesus, and properly documented their interpretation, and the African Orthodox Church emerged as the true church of the black man."[19]

The new church operated much like the Roman Catholic Church, borrowing many of its rites and rituals. "The Holy Trinity [was] acknowledged—in black, of course. An impressive ceremony was held at Liberty Hall, and a 'Special Form of Divine Service' was performed . . . for the purpose of 'canonization' of the Lord Jesus Christ as 'the Black Man of Sorrow' and the Blessed Virgin Mary as a Black Madonna."[20]

In keeping with his call for all blacks to come together as a nation, Garvey held what he called the first "Universal Negro

Marcus Garvey, leader of the the back-to-Africa movement.

Convention" in Harlem. At the convention, delegates adopted a flag of red, black, and green, to represent a provisional black government to be established in Africa. After the sessions, members of the UNIA, wearing military-style uniforms, poured out onto the streets and paraded through Harlem accompanied by marching bands and singing choruses.

The convention, parades, and Garvey's influential *Negro World* brought attention to Garvey and to his movement, but not all the attention was good. The Black Star Line failed, and Garvey was arrested on charges of mail fraud. He was convicted and sentenced to five years in jail. Two years after his conviction, President Calvin Coolidge pardoned him, and he was deported back to Jamaica as an undesirable alien. Without his leadership, the UNIA fell apart. Garvey died in obscurity in London in 1940, having never made it to Africa.

Though his movement failed, Garvey left an indelible mark on the lives of African Americans. According to Ottley, "Concretely, the movement set in motion what was to become the most compelling force in Negro life—race and color consciousness, which is today that ephemeral thing that inspires 'race loyalty'; the banner to which Negroes rally; the chain that binds them together."[21]

Garvey did not consider himself a failure. "Be assured that I planted well the seed of Negro or black nationalism that cannot be destroyed."[22] Garvey did indeed plant the seed of black nationalism. His emphasis on black pride and self-help, and his focus on the people, history, and culture of Africa influenced black leaders of the twentieth century, especially those in the Nation of Islam.

The Nation of Islam

The Nation of Islam (NOI), founded in Detroit, Michigan, in 1931 by Wallace D. Fard, found favor with working-class African Americans living in the North. Walking the streets of Detroit, Fard proclaimed the superiority of the black race. He preached a blend of traditional Islam and antiwhite sentiment. Frustrated with established Christian churches' inability to bring about change in their lives, people were drawn to Fard and to his message. When Fard mysteriously departed in 1934, Elijah Muhammad became head of the organization. He used many of Marcus Garvey's UNIA tactics to attract members.

Although Elijah Muhammad preached black nationalist ideology, he did not see the need to move back to Africa, as Garvey did. Instead, the NOI demanded land in the southern United States to found a black nation. The organization felt the requested land would serve as restitution for the economic and social injustice of

Elijah Muhammad (1897–1975)

Born Elijah Poole outside Macon, Georgia, in 1897, he grew up in a family of thirteen children. His parents were sharecroppers. His father was also a minister. Poole completed only three years of school before he had to work to help support his family. At sixteen, he married and moved to

Detroit. There, he heard Wallace Fard preach and became a disciple of the Nation of Islam. The NOI leader took Poole as a student and gave him a new last name— Muhammad. Elijah Muhammad became a leader of the Temple of Islam. When Fard disappeared in 1934, Elijah Muhammad became NOI's leader and continued in that position until his death in 1975.

Elijah Muhammad.

slavery. Elijah Muhammad's nationalism was loosely based on the religion of Islam, but it also contained an antiwhite ideology that appealed to poor urban blacks. The organization taught the need for self-discipline, responsibility, and self-sufficiency. In keeping with the organization's teachings of racial self-sufficiency, the NOI created farms and businesses to help break the dependency on whites.

While leading the NOI, Elijah Muhammad preached the importance of traditional values of Islam, opposed drugs and alcohol, nurtured ghetto small businesses and reached out to criminals. One of those to whom he reached out was an ex-convict with cinnamon-colored hair, known on the streets as "Detroit Red." That young man eventually rose in the organization and took the name Malcolm X.

Malcolm X, as a spokesman for the Nation of Islam, initially opposed the nonviolent tactics of Martin Luther King, Jr. and the mainstream civil rights movement.

Born Malcolm Little in Omaha, Nebraska, in 1925, his parents had been profoundly influenced by Marcus Garvey's movement. Earl Little, Malcolm's father, was a preacher who was active in the UNIA. His support of Garveyism elicited death threats from white supremacy groups in Omaha, so the Littles moved to Michigan to escape the threats. However, the danger followed them, and several years later, Earl Little's mutilated body was found on the trolley tracks. Police ruled the death accidental, but the Little family knew better. This early tragedy showed Malcolm how dangerous the life of a civil rights leader could be, but it did not prevent him from eventually taking up the cause.

Malcolm X's eventual celebrity as leader and spokesman of the Nation of Islam brought him into the spotlight. His disagreement with the central goals of the mainstream Civil Rights Movement of the 1950s and 1960s, and in particular of the nonviolent efforts of Martin Luther King Jr. as leader of the movement, demonstrated a basic difference in the desires and needs of middle-class and lower-class blacks.

Chapter Four

The Civil Rights Era

Martin Luther King's nonviolent protest movement and the more militant approaches of radical black leaders like Malcolm X may have taken center stage in America in the 1960s, but theirs were not the first efforts toward integration or racial equality in the twentieth century. In the years following World War I, activists tried to achieve some semblance of equality, but their efforts faced stiff resistance. In the mid-twentieth century, after World War II, efforts toward black nationalism met with somewhat more success, and it was those smaller victories that led to the more widely known movement of King and the notoriety of Malcolm X.

Early Protests

Public protests against racial discrimination began early in the twentieth century. After the stock market crash in 1929, African Americans protested against businesses that would not hire them because of their race. Protesters and picket lines first appeared in Chicago, Illinois, and then spread to other major cities. The slogan on many picket signs read, "Don't Buy Where You Can't Work." Protests against segregationist hiring practices continued in 1941. In that year New York City bus companies

Asa Philip Randolph (1889–1979)

Born the son of an African Methodist Episcopal minister in Crescent City, Florida, in 1889, A. Philip Randolph eventually became one of America's most influential black leaders. In 1917 he cofounded the *Messenger*, a radical Socialist weekly that campaigned against lynching and encouraged its readers to oppose the U.S. entry into World War I and to refuse to enlist to fight to preserve this country's segregated society. In 1925 he organized the nation's first black labor union, the Brotherhood of Sleeping Car Porters and Maids (BSCP). In 1936 he cofounded the National Negro Congress, a loose coalition of 585 organizations whose shared aims were equal treatment for blacks, and for that matter, for workers of all races. In 1940 and 1941, pressure from Randolph forced President Franklin Roosevelt to sign an order prohibiting racial discrimination in federal hiring. While forming the BSCP, Randolph came to oppose the motives and practices of Marcus Garvey. According to Randolph, "What you needed to follow Garvey was a leap of the imagination, but socialism and trade unionism called for rigorous social struggle—hard work and programs—and few people wanted to think about that. Against the emotional power of Garveyism, what I was preaching didn't stand a chance." Instead of the pomp, display, and what he felt were the empty promises of Garvey, Randolph advocated mass demonstrations, boycotts, the wide distribution of antidiscrimination pamphlets, and legal action to achieve his goals.

On August 28, 1963, at the age of seventy-four, and more than twenty years after his threatened march on Washington, A. Philip Randolph stood before a crowd of 250,000 before the Lincoln Memorial in Washington, D.C., to introduce a young Martin Luther King Jr., about to deliver his "I Have a Dream" speech at the culmination of the epochal March on Washington.

Quoted in Columbus Salley, *The Black 100: A Ranking of the Most Influential African-Americans, Past and Present.* New York: Citadel, 1993, p. 123.

A. Philip Randolph.

refused to hire black drivers or mechanics, so African Americans stayed off city buses for four weeks. The loss of income from the decrease in riders eventually forced the companies to change their hiring policies.

U.S. president Franklin Delano Roosevelt (1882–1945) talked about the importance of civil rights but took little action unless forced to do so. In 1941 Asa Philip Randolph, head of the National Negro Congress, an organization whose aim was the liberation of blacks and the end of discrimination, called for a hundred-thousand-person march on Washington. The threat of such a large demonstration in Washington on the Fourth of July was enough to goad Roosevelt into action. He signed Executive Order 8802 in June 1941, forbidding racial discrimination in hiring for government projects and defense industries.

Another organization that had its origins in the 1940s was CORE, the Congress of Racial Equality. Founded in Chicago in 1942 by James Farmer and an interracial group of activists, it led early protests against racial discrimination in hiring. CORE vowed to take direct action against discriminatory practices in public places, housing, and services.

The "separate but equal" concept codified discrimination—it made it law. But in truth, accommodations might be separate, but they were rarely equal. By the 1950s black organizations such as the NAACP and CORE turned their attention to the unequal treatment African Americans received as a result of the *Plessy v. Ferguson* decision of the Supreme Court.

Fighting Against *Plessy*

Inequality between blacks and whites had existed in the United States for centuries. The concept of "separate but equal," as officially established in the U.S. Supreme Court's ruling in *Plessy v. Ferguson* in 1896, had gone unchallenged since it was implemented. In the Court's ruling, separate accommodations for the races were deemed not only acceptable, but the law of the land. For fifty years, *Plessy* empowered whites to discriminate against blacks, effectively dooming them to second-class citizenship.

Where the inequities of "separate but equal" became most visible were in the cases of black soldiers, who had fought for the United States in two world wars, coming home to a nation that treated them as less than equal. In one notable case, a World War II veteran—a black soldier—was returning home by army bus. He "took too long" at a rest stop, which irritated the driver, and he was beaten into blindness because of his slowness. This soldier's story became national news when the NAACP used it to lobby for effective civil rights. As a result, membership in the NAACP increased rapidly, and African Americans decided enough was enough. The time had come for change, and that change came in the form of legal action on behalf of black schoolchildren.

In Topeka, Kansas, in 1951, Oliver Brown and thirteen other black parents brought a class-action suit against the city's board of education, claiming racial discrimination. The Browns lived in an integrated neighborhood, and their daughter played with children of several different races. But Linda Brown was not allowed to attend the elementary school seven blocks from her family home. Only white students could enroll there. Linda had to walk six blocks to a bus that would take her more than a mile away to a school for black students. Linda wanted to go to school with her friends but was denied entrance to the all-white school in her neighborhood.

Upon hearing the case, the district court in Kansas ruled in favor of the board of education, citing the U.S. Supreme Court decision in *Plessy v. Ferguson* that established the concept of "separate but equal." Brown did not give up. Instead, he requested help from the NAACP's Legal Defense Fund, under the leadership of Thurgood Marshall (1908–1993). Marshall took the case. He and a team of lawyers combined the Brown case with four other lawsuits against segregated school districts in various U.S. cities into what was officially called *Brown v. Board of Education*. In 1952 the NAACP team presented their arguments to the U.S. Supreme Court.

On May 17, 1954, the Court ruled in their favor—to overturn *Plessy* and thus end legal segregation in the United States. In delivering the Court's unanimous ruling, Chief Justice Earl Warren wrote:

We come then to the question presented: Does segregation of children in public schools solely on the basis of race,

even though the physical facilities and other "tangible" factors may be equal, deprive the children of the minority group of equal educational opportunities? We believe it does. . . . We conclude that in the field of public education the doctrine of "separate but equal" has no place. Separate educational facilities are inherently unequal. Therefore, we hold that the plaintiffs . . . [have been] deprived of the equal protection of the laws guaranteed by the Fourteenth Amendment.[23]

The ruling, which took years to fully implement, strengthened the "integrationist" position in black nationalist thinking. The *Brown* case demonstrated that blacks could win their legal rights through the U.S. court system. The decision opened the door for social change in the country.

Change came slowly, however, and delays inspired protests. And the protests ushered in the fourth period of intense black nationalism thinking and action. By this time, the nationalist ideas espoused by Marcus Garvey in the 1920s had

Students represented in the *Brown v. Board of Education* case, with their parents.

53

become a part of African American thinking. His insistence on black separation, pride, and the beauty of the race gave African Americans the courage to step into the public arena to demand their rights. The relative success of Garvey's parades and speeches at gaining attention to his cause taught black leaders that public displays could bring attention to their cause as well.

Nonviolent Activism

Black nationalist ideology stood at the center of the Civil Rights Movement, but again, it had two sides. Some black nationalists advocated immediate and often violent protests and demonstrations to gain African American civil rights. Others believed nonviolent action would bring about the change, even though it might take longer. Those who called for change "by any means necessary" were usually separatists. They advocated complete separation of the races in all things. Those who favored nonviolence were "integrationist," working toward the goal of equal rights for all under the U.S. Constitution.

The nonviolent action taken during the Civil Rights Movement came in the form of legal challenges, civil protests, and public demonstrations. African Americans risked their money, lives, and honor to achieve equality in the United States. This time, however, they were not alone. White college students, intellectuals, and religious leaders joined what became known simply as "the movement," and Martin Luther King Jr. was recognized as its leader.

The movement began in reaction to Southern states' reluctance to integrate their schools after the *Brown* decision. Soon protests addressed other "separate but equal" issues, such as segregated seating on buses, at lunch counters, and in movie theaters. On December 1, 1955, a tired black workingwoman in Montgomery, Alabama—Rosa Parks—climbed aboard a city bus and sat down in the first seat she found—at the front of the vehicle. Blacks were supposed to sit in the back, so when the bus got crowded, the driver asked Parks to give up her seat to a white man. She refused. The police were called, and she was arrested.

Rosa Parks was not the first African American to be arrested for refusing to take her place at the back of the bus. It was, however, the first time such an arrest made news. Thousands of

Rosa Parks (right) refused to give up her seat on a Montgomery, Alabama, bus to a white man. Her subsequent arrest sparked the boycott that eventually resulted in the desegregation of city transportation.

African Americans in Montgomery stopped riding the buses. For over a year, they walked to work, to school, and to the store. The well-organized boycott forced the city to desegregate seating in the buses. Martin Luther King Jr. provided leadership for this early protest.

The Montgomery bus boycott sent a clear message that African Americans would no longer accept their "place" as second-class citizens. Two years later, in 1957, the president of the United States made it clear the nation would not accept it either. Orval Faubus, the governor of Arkansas, defied a federal court order and refused to integrate the state's public schools. The governor called out the state National Guard to keep black students out of the all-white Little Rock High School. President Dwight Eisenhower federalized the state's National Guard and called in additional federal troops to protect the black students entering the white high school.

Further Steps to Freedom

The incident in Arkansas made news all over the country. Soon, newspaper stories and the nightly television news reports were

Martin Luther King Jr.

Martin Luther King Jr. (1929–1968) was born in Atlanta, Georgia, to a Baptist preacher and his wife. In fact, he came from a family of preachers. Both of his grandfathers were Baptist ministers. Grandfather King began the family's long tenure as pastors of Ebenezer Baptist Church in Atlanta. After obtaining a doctor of divinity degree from Boston University, King took a position as pastor to a church in Montgomery, Alabama. His civil rights efforts began there—with the Montgomery bus boycott.

In 1957 he formed the Southern Christian Leadership Conference (SCLC) and began speaking across the country, advocating nonviolent action to achieve civil rights for African Americans. He returned to Atlanta in 1960 to become co-pastor at Ebenezer. He helped organize the 1963 March on Washington. The march influenced the passage of the Civil Rights Act of 1964. His civil rights activism gained him many enemies, and he was assassinated in Memphis, Tennessee, in 1968.

full of stories about civil rights protests. College students inspired by the human rights stories joined the protests. In 1960 African American college students sat down at a segregated lunch counter in Greensboro, North Carolina. When they ordered food, they broke that state's segregation law. They were attacked by white high school students but returned the following day and were joined by other college students, white as well as black. The lunch counter story appeared in the *New York Times*, drawing national attention. More lunch counter sit-ins followed.

College students from across the country also participated in "freedom rides." The Congress of Racial Equality (CORE) sent black and white students—"freedom riders"—together on bus trips through the South to test whether the laws against segregated interstate transportation were being honored. The brutal attacks they suffered at the hands of white mobs, while local lawmen stood idly by, proved that those laws were not being enforced.

To show the level of African American support for the Civil Rights Movement, King helped organize a march on Washington in 1963. Television images of 250,000 people, most of them African Americans, peacefully gathered around the Reflecting Pool in the nation's capital sent the message across the country. King's speech was no less impressive. In it, he outlined his dream for his children, his race, and his nation:

> I say to you today my friends, even though we face the dif-
> ficulties of today and tomorrow, I still have a dream. It is a
> dream deeply rooted in the American dream. I have a
> dream that one day this nation will rise up and live out the
> true meaning of its creed: "We hold these truths to be self-
> evident, that all men are created equal." . . . I have a dream
> that my four little children will one day live in a nation
> where they will not be judged by the color of their skin but
> by the content of their character."[24]

A year after King's "I Have a Dream" speech, civil rights groups gathered in Mississippi to register African American voters. Many Southern whites objected to what they called "outside agitators." Three young civil rights workers disappeared, one black and two white. Their bodies were not found until President Lyndon Johnson sent federal troops to search for them. The bodies of James

Martin Luther King Jr. waves to the crowd gathered at the Lincoln Memorial to hear his now-famous "I Have a Dream" speech.

Earl Chaney, Andrew Goodman, and Michael Schwerner were finally discovered where they had been hastily buried under an earthen dam in rural Neshoba County, Mississippi, on the night of June 20, 1964.

Two months later, President Johnson signed the historic Civil Rights Act of 1964. It prohibits discrimination in federally assisted government programs and protects the constitutional rights of all races in public facilities and public education. Despite the president's efforts, however, the violence did not end. On March 7, 1965, civil rights activists planned a voting rights march from Selma, Alabama, to the state's capitol in Montgomery. When marchers reached the Edmund Pettus Bridge, state troopers ordered them to stop and disperse. The protesters were not given a chance to react. They were attacked with tear gas, whips, and clubs. Fifty protesters were hospitalized in that nationally televised debacle.

After Selma, more marches were organized. King led a march two days later, and more followed. Television cameras, of course, recorded the events, allowing the whole country to witness what was happening in the South. Americans, watching civil rights protests and the violent response they elicited, wondered if the nation might be on the brink of another civil war.

Alabama state troopers confront civil rights demonstrators in a cloud of tear gas in Selma, Alabama, in 1965.

"We Shall Overcome!"

As protesters marched in Alabama, Johnson addressed a joint session of Congress to urge them to pass the Voting Rights Act. The president's televised speech enabled him to appeal not only to Congress, but to the nation as well:

> There is no Negro problem. There is no Southern problem. There is no Northern problem. There is only an American problem . . . and we are met here as Americans to solve that problem. . . . But even if we pass this bill the battle will not be over. What happened in Selma is part of a far larger movement which reaches into every section and state of America. It is the effort of American Negroes to secure for themselves the full blessings of American life. Their cause must be our cause too. Because it's not just Negroes, but really it is all of us, who must overcome the crippling legacy of bigotry and injustice. And we shall overcome.[25]

Johnson's speech echoed a line from a popular civil rights anthem. His appeal helped ensure the passage of the voting rights legislation, outlawing literacy tests and other requirements that restricted African American voting.

As an "integrationist," King believed the nonviolent protests would bring change and end segregation. He also hoped it would put an end to the violence black people faced, not just in the South, but all over the country. His dedication to the Civil Rights Movement, however, ended violently on April 4, 1968, when he was shot while standing outside his room at the Lorraine Motel in Memphis, Tennessee. His assassination sparked riots in 130 cities around the country. King had tried to work within the system to bring equal treatment for African Americans. There were those, however, who disagreed with his tactics.

By Any Means Necessary

Where King's version of black nationalism took an integrationist approach (which appealed to middle-class blacks), the views of Malcolm X were separatist, appealing instead to working-class and poor blacks of the inner cities. His black nationalism largely rejected the nonviolence of the Civil Rights Movement, recognizing instead that violence in the struggle for black freedom and independence was sometimes necessary.

Malcolm pointed out that white supremacists had used violence to deny civil rights to blacks, and that blacks should therefore be free to respond to violence in kind. In an interview with psychologist and author Kenneth B. Clark, he explained his reasoning:

> Any human being who is intelligent has the right to defend himself. You can't take a black man who is being bitten by dogs and accuse him of advocating violence because he tries to defend himself from the bite of the dog. . . . Any Negro who teaches Negroes to turn the other cheek in the face of attack is disarming that Negro of his God-given right, of his moral right, of his natural right, of his intelligent right to defend himself.[26]

In another speech, known as "Message to the Grass Roots," delivered in Detroit, Michigan, on November 10, 1963, Malcolm compared violence on U.S. streets to violence in the Vietnam War, making his position even clearer:

> If violence is wrong in America, violence is wrong abroad. If it is wrong to be violent defending black women and black children and black babies and black men, then it is wrong for America to draft us and make us violent abroad in defense of her. And if it is right for America to draft us, and teach us how to be violent in defense of her, then it is right for you and me to do whatever is necessary to defend our own people right here in this country.[27]

It was a clear warning—and a threat. When Malcolm Little first joined the Nation of Islam in 1952 and changed his name to Malcolm X, his black nationalist thinking was "separatist." He thought of whites as devils, and his speeches reflected that philosophy. His words were meant to irritate whites and inspire blacks, and they did just that. Whites thought of him as a rabble-rouser and a troublemaker who would cause dissatisfaction among blacks that could lead to possibly violent public demonstrations. Blacks saw him as a charismatic leader who could help the cause for civil rights.

Nation of Islam leader Malcolm X, pictured, was not opposed to the use of violence in the fight for African Americans' civil rights.

Malcolm X's separatist nationalism stood in stark contrast to King's mainstream black nationalism. It was, however, a calculated move, as he confessed to King's wife. After delivering one of his frank speeches in Selma, Alabama, Malcolm X took his seat next to Mrs. King and apologized: "I want [King] to know that I didn't come here to make his job more difficult; I thought that if the white people understood what the alternative was, that they would be willing to listen to Dr. King."[28] Malcolm X's call for change "by any means necessary" inspired many. His views stood in sharp contrast to King's, but Malcolm's life ended as King's had, at the hand of an assassin. He was gunned down as he began to speak at the Audubon Ballroom in Harlem, on February 21, 1965.

Other Militant Groups

Other groups with separatist black nationalist ideas were also founded during the 1960s. One of these was the Student Nonviolent Coordinating Committee (SNCC, called "Snick"), founded in 1960. Its main purpose was to help college students organize and participate in public protests against segregation in the South. SNCC, like the NAACP, welcomed white student members. The organizing meeting had been called by Ella Baker, an official of King's Southern Christian Leadership Conference (SCLC). King and other civil rights leaders hoped SNCC would serve as the youth wing of the SCLC, but the student group remained fiercely independent.

At first, SNCC, like the SCLC, was committed to nonviolent direct-action public protests to counter white prejudice. The violence in Selma, Alabama, however, redirected SNCC's focus. The youth organization elected Stokely Carmichael as its chairman, and he moved the group away from nonviolence and interracial cooperation. Instead, he began using the term "black power" and seemed to reject the nonviolent methods of the mainstream Civil Rights Movement.

Whites were alarmed by the term. They perceived it as a threat of black supremacy rather than white supremacy—possibly even a threat of a race war—and Carmichael was asked repeatedly to define what he meant by it. Finally, in a 1967 interview for *Life* magazine, Carmichael said:

For the last time, "Black Power" means black people coming together to form a political force and either electing representatives or forcing their representatives to speak their needs [rather than relying on established parties]. "Black Power" doesn't mean anti-white, violence, separatism or any other racist things the press says it means. It's saying "Look buddy, we're not laying a vote on you unless you lay so many schools, hospitals, playgrounds and good jobs on us."[29]

A group that took Carmichael's "black power" to heart, as well as Malcolm X's call to use "whatever means necessary" was the Black Panther Party (BPP). Huey P. Newton and Bobby Seale founded the organization in Oakland, California, in the mid-1960s. It soon expanded to other large cities across the country. Organized in the manner of a paramilitary group, members wore black berets and patches on clothing to identify themselves.

BPP opposed police brutality and organized neighborhood patrols in major cities that followed police officers to ensure against race-related arrests or harassment. This idea for neighborhood patrols was originally used by Carmichael in rural Alabama. As a result of their presence, several major city police departments hired significantly more African American officers. Despite the good that came of their actions, clashes between armed Black Panthers and police resulted in deaths on both sides.

Black Power

Amid those isolated in American inner cities in the 1970s, 1980s, and 1990s, integration meant little, but "black power" meant everything. Nonviolent civil rights protests were no longer in the news. They had been replaced with stories of black militancy—race riots, charges of police brutality, and stories of black-on-black violence which happened as a result of crushing poverty and widespread drug use. To many suburban whites, the problems of urban blacks began to seem distant, so efforts to correct them lost their popular appeal.

Legislation had changed the laws relating to race, but no one was able to completely change people's attitudes toward race. According to black activist, former member of SNCC and BPP,

Stokely Carmichael, shown speaking, steered the Student Nonviolent Coordinating Committee toward a platform based on black power.

and law professor Kathleen Cleaver in a 1997 interview for *Front-line*, a PBS documentary program:

> By the time the Civil Rights Act of 1964 and the Voting Rights Act of 1965 were passed by the United States Congress, the process of legal change and elimination of official racism was legally completed, but it was not socially completed. The government that was interested in encouraging the end of restrictions on voting and education on the basis of race didn't do very much on the level of changing basic attitudes. So where you have a cessation of the implementation by law of racist practices, you really have never seen any major effort on the part of the government or the larger institutions to transform attitudes. And that is where we've failed.[30]

Black power advocates in the 1960s and 1970s, however, were not interested in changing the attitudes of white Americans. They wanted "effective control and self-determination by men of color in their own areas. Power is total control of the economic, polit-

Stokely Carmichael (1941–1998)

Born in Port of Spain, Trinidad, Stokely Carmichael came to the United States with his family at the age of eleven. He lived in a mostly white, middle-class neighborhood in New York City and went to the Bronx High School of Science. As a student at Howard University in Washington, D.C., he joined the civil rights movement. Carmichael participated in the freedom rides organized by CORE in 1961, and then went on to work in other civil rights demonstrations across the South.

When Mississippi black activist James Meredith was shot while attempting a one-man protest march across the South to spur voter registration, Carmichael joined Martin Luther King Jr. and others to complete Meredith's planned walk. He was arrested and went to jail. He had been arrested twenty-six times before, but this time was different. He emerged from jail a committed "separatist." He coined the slogan "Black Is Beautiful" and advocated the concept of black power. In 1969 he moved to Ghana and changed his name to Kwame Ture. He died in 1998.

ical, educational, and social life of our community from the top to the bottom."[31] This definition came from the 1966 Black Power Conference organized by U.S. Congressman Adam Clayton Powell from Harlem. The idea was later refined as the "Four Ends of Black Power" at the final Black Power Conference, held in 1970. There, the goals of black power were listed as self-determination, self-sufficiency, self-respect, and self-defense for black Americans.

Chapter Five

Black Nationalism and Popular Culture

"Black power" for a time replaced "black nationalism" as a term for racial solidarity. During the civil rights era, images of black power advocates appeared regularly on nightly newscasts. Black power activists such as Stokely Carmichael and Angela Davis wore African-inspired clothing and hair styles. This inspired young people of all races and brought African fashions into popular culture. The clothing included the caftan, a long robelike garment worn by women, and the dashiki, a short robelike garment worn as a shirt by men. Kente cloth, a multi-colored woven cloth that originated in Ghana, was adopted by African Americans as a sign of their connection to Africa and soon became popular. The cloth was used not only in clothing, but for handbags, luggage, and upholstery.

Within a few years, people of all ages and races in the United States had adopted the comfortable, colorful clothing style worn by black power activists. When this happened, some black activists resented it. Angela Davis, a Black Panther advocate, wore her hair in a natural style in the 1960s and 1970s that created what looked like a bubble or halo of black around her head. Her image can still be seen on posters in dorm rooms on college campuses, but, according to her, the image sent a wrong message: "I am remembered as a hairdo. It is humiliating because it reduces a politics of liberation to a politics of fashion."[32]

When dashikis, caftans, and afros entered the worlds of fashion and hairstyle, they brought African culture with them. Some blacks were pleased that examples of their heritage were gaining popularity, but others believed their cross-cultural popularity took African-inspired fashions away from blacks as a unique expression of their racial identity.

Unlike these popular trends, Kwanzaa, the 1966 brainchild of California State–Long Beach professor Maulana Karenga, remains a largely African American celebration. The nonreligious holiday takes place each year between Christmas and New Year, and its aim is to instill community values and reinforce the connection between African Americans and their African roots. Today, more than forty years after its inception, Karenga's holiday creation continues to grow in popularity.

African-inspired clothing and celebrations brought a demand for more information about the continent and the people that originated there. Colleges and universities developed Black Studies programs and degrees. This concentration on Africa brought a reexamination of what black people called themselves. At first, it was "colored," then "Negro." In the 1960s the "Black Is Beautiful" slogan of black power advocates demanded that the term be

Kwanzaa

---◼---

Celebrated annually from December 26 to January 1, Kwanzaa is based on the themes of traditional harvest rituals common to a number of African peoples. It emphasizes human dignity, the well-being of the family, and the human connection to nature and the environment.

The holiday was created by Maulana Karenga, a black studies professor at California State University at Long Beach, and was first observed in 1966. The term "Kwanzaa" comes from a Swahili word meaning "first fruits." The holiday, though not religious (as are Christmas and Hanukkah), aims to reinforce community values and strengthen African cultural identity.

"black." Since 1988, however, there has been a social and political movement to officially adopt "African American." According to Reverend Jesse Jackson, civil rights leader and one-time candidate for president:

Just as we were called colored, but were not that, and then Negro, but [were] not that, to be called black is just as baseless. To be called African-Americans has cultural integrity. It puts us in our proper historical context. Every ethnic group in this country has a reference to some land base, some historical cultural base. African-Americans have hit that level of cultural maturity. There are Armenian-Americans and Jewish-Americans and Arab-Americans and Italian-Americans. And with a degree of accepted and reasonable pride, they connect their heritage to their mother country and where they are now.[33]

"African American" thus embraces both the continent of origin for the race and the nation that members of the race call home.

News providers, both print and broadcast, were quick to note the name change. Though images of African

Many African Americans celebrate the holiday of Kwanzaa as a nonreligious holiday intended to reinforce community values.

American protestors appeared often on news broadcasts during the civil rights era, black people were seldom featured on prime-time entertainment shows.

Black Pioneers on Network Television

Prior to the civil rights era, virtually all blacks who appeared on TV were either cast as domestics, farm workers, or in other servile roles. These roles were almost always played for laughs. One exception was the short-lived variety show featuring Nat "King" Cole, a popular black singer, which aired on NBC from 1956 to 1957. Lack of advertising caused the show to be canceled. Advertisers did not think television viewers wanted to see a show headed by a black man.

Why not? Research on television viewers and viewing patterns showed that the largest part of the television audience was middle-class and white. Advertisers, therefore, would not sponsor shows that featured black actors. This began to change after the Civil Rights Movement of the 1960s.

The first black actor to appear in a realistic dramatic role was Bill Cosby. He costarred with Robert Culp in the NBC series *I Spy*, which ran from 1965 to 1968. Cosby's role as a black international spy and partner to Culp's white character depicted him as extremely well educated, suave, and self-confident. Cosby's acting earned him Emmy Awards three years in a row.

The first black woman in a dramatic TV role was Nichelle Nichols, who played Lieutenant Uhura, the communications officer aboard the starship *Enterprise* on the series *Star Trek*. The series ran from 1966 to 1969, also on NBC. Though not a starring role, her portrayal as an equal on the bridge of the *Enterprise* opened the door for other actresses, most notably Diahann Carroll, who starred in her own situation comedy *Julia*, from 1968 to 1971, again on NBC. Carroll played an independent single mom, living and working in a fully integrated section of Los Angeles. Julia, however, lived a middle-class lifestyle that looked more white than black.

The success of these shows proved to advertisers that television programs with primary black characters could attract large audiences. The success of *Julia* encouraged networks to offer more programs featuring blacks, but most continued to portray black life as

Nichelle Nichols became the first black woman in a dramatic television role when she played Lieutenant Uhura on the popular 1960s series *Star Trek*.

comedy rather than serious drama. *The Jeffersons* (1975–1985), *Good Times* (1974–1979), *What's Happening!!* (1976–1979), and *Diff'rent Strokes* (1978–1985) were examples of that trend.

As entertaining as the shows were, black nationalist ideas rarely found an effective platform on TV. Comedy provides entertainment, but dramatic shows depicting black nationalist issues might frighten white, middle-class viewers, or so television advertisers thought. Two landmark television productions in the mid-1970s, however, showcased black actors in realistic portrayals of life as African Americans before and during the Jim Crow era. These shows clearly addressed black nationalist issues.

In 1974 Cicely Tyson led a mostly black cast in the TV movie *The Autobiography of Miss Jane Pittman*, the story of an old black Southern woman who had lived from the days of slavery until the civil rights era. Tyson won acclaim for her stellar performance. The landmark black television production, however, was *Roots*. In 1977 ABC aired this miniseries, which was based on the book by Alex Haley. It told the story of several generations of a black family—from life in Africa to slavery in the American South, to freedom, to racial discrimination during the Jim Crow era, and then to modern times. *Roots* opened white eyes to the ordeals blacks had suffered at the hands of whites for generations, forever changing the way many white Americans perceived blacks.

Roots also opened the eyes of television advertisers. The miniseries captured thirty-four Emmy Award nominations and won nine. It attracted a huge audience that currently stands as the third highest-rated show in television history behind the *M*A*S*H* finale and Super Bowl XLII.

In 1984 a realistically portrayed upper-middle-class urban black family appeared on national television, starring black television pioneer Bill Cosby. Advertisers had noticed that their favorite audience—the middle class—by then contained a large number of blacks. Cosby's show played to this new audience. Billed as a "domestic comedy," the show followed the life and times of the Huxtables, a black upper-middle-class family—Mom a lawyer and Dad a doctor—living in a fashionable Brooklyn, New York, townhouse.

The Cosby Show became a huge hit, and advertisers were delighted. The show, however, still cast African American life as

The Cosby Show, which began its television run in 1984, appealed to a middle-class audience composed of both whites and blacks.

comedy, despite the Huxtables sometimes dealing with serious family issues. Network television still did not provide much programming for an expanding middle-class black audience. The success of *The Cosby Show*, however, may have helped to bring advertisers to a new television network aimed at a predominantly black audience.

BET—Black Entertainment Television

Started on a small scale in 1980, Black Entertainment Television, or BET, has become the longest-running television network aimed specifically at an African American audience. However, despite its pioneering effort, it now attracts critics from both races.

Founded by Robert L. Johnson, BET began as a two-hour Friday night block on the USA network. Showing mostly older movies and music videos, it attracted a small but loyal following. In 1983, with funding from Home Box Office (HBO), BET launched a twenty-four hour schedule, featuring situation comedies, African American dramatic series, music shows (primarily

In 1980 Robert L. Johnson founded Black Entertainment Television, or BET.

hip-hop), and religious programming. It also aired specials of interest to the African American community as well as a daily newscast.

With a viewing audience of 7.6 million subscribers, this cable channel would seem to be quite popular, and it is. However, it has also earned harsh criticism for its programming choices and its marketing practices. Many prominent critics, including rapper Chuck D (of Public Enemy) and film director Spike Lee, claim the network is more interested in making a profit than in focusing on issues important to the black community. Others have criticized BET for its dramatic and comedy series, saying they tend to perpetuate racial stereotypes.

Some were critical of the network for airing rap artists whose language and message were not appropriate for younger viewers. (BET has since begun censoring such language in its music videos.) Finally, some disagree with BET's religious programming, saying either that the views expressed are not inclusive of many African Americans or that the ministers featured are known to be less than ethical in their ministries. Critics have been fairly outspoken about the network in the past few years, joking that BET actually stands for "Black Exploitation Television" and that they consider it a modern-day minstrel show.

Television programming continues to be aimed at the middle class, both white and black. Poor people are rarely seen outside of police dramas where they are portrayed as either criminals or victims. Music channels, such as VH1 and MTV, as well as BET, though, are able to display conditions and issues relating to inner cities through music videos. Beginning in 1981 with the appearance of MTV, television music channels introduced hip-hop music and images related to urban blacks to a national and international audience.

The hip-hop culture may not have a high profile on television, but it dominates the music business. This music rose out of black and Puerto Rican neighborhoods in New York City. Lyrics of this music reflect the anger and isolation felt by young people living in those neighborhoods. Separation from whites is one of the major points of black nationalist thinking, and poor urban blacks not only advocate that separation, they live it, making black nationalism a major part of the music genre called hip-hop.

Four main elements of hip-hop—deejaying, rapping, break dancing, and graffiti—give inner-city teens opportunities to express themselves. For teens who often feel disconnected from mainstream American society and who feel largely voiceless as well as powerless, hip-hop gives them that voice, allowing them to express their frustrations about being poor—and about being black—in America. In short, it helps them express their own version of black nationalism.

Break dancing and graffiti contests also give young people a chance to work off excess energy in a positive way. Some believe early hip-hop music actually helped reduce inner-city violence. Tony Tone, of the rap group Cold Crush Brothers, contends, "Hip-hop saved a lot of lives."[34]

Deejaying

Clive Campbell, a Jamaican disc jockey, brought the Jamaican tradition of "toasting"—off-the-cuff poetry or sayings performed with reggae, funk, or some other type of music playing in the background—to New York City. Campbell, who went by the name "Kool Herc," was also the first in the United States to use a technique called "break-beat deejaying"—playing repetitive, highly danceable segments of songs for all-night dance parties.

Later, Grandmaster Flash expanded the art form. Known as one of the founding fathers of hip-hop, Grandmaster Flash developed most of the turntable techniques employed by hip-hop artists today. In addition to "cutting" (using two turntables and moving between tracks exactly on the beat), "back-spinning" (manually turning records to repeat brief snippets of sound), and "phasing" (manipulating turntable speeds), he also used "scratching"—moving a record back and forth under a needle to produce the rhythmic, jarring sound that has come to be one of the primary characteristics of hip-hop and rap music.

Rap

The term "rap" originally meant to hit or strike an object, but it later developed into a slang term for lengthy informal discussions about topics of interest. Used extensively by African Americans in the 1960s, "rap" came to be associated with hip-hop music in the 1970s, due to its use of impromptu poetry chanted to a beat. Rap

DJ Grandmaster Flash is considered one of the founding fathers of hip-hop and the art of deejaying.

Break Dancing

▬

Break dancing developed as a part of the hip-hop music scene, providing another avenue for self-expression for black teens. The freestyle moves of the dance are performed to breaks in music created by a deejay's manipulating records between songs. Deejay-created turntable techniques such as cutting, back phasing, spinning, and scratching created a rhythm-only section between musical numbers. Dancers would fill this "break" in the music with freestyle dance moves. These moves are varied and require imagination, coordination, and a good deal of athleticism.

The dance has no set series of moves. Each dancer creates a unique performance. This is what has made break dancing a competition. Rival youth groups can face off against each other at hip-hop dance parties instead of in gang violence on the street.

owes its origin to griots, or folk poets of West Africa, who began telling stories to drumbeats centuries before the United States was formed. Another tradition that may have its origin in West Africa is the African American practice of exchanging verbal and sometimes rhyming insults called "the dozens," which has also played a part in rap music.

Early rap artists such as Public Enemy and X-Clan promoted strong black nationalistic messages, but by the mid-1990s, rap lyrics and their message had shifted largely to materialism—focusing on wealth and prestige rather than social issues. The late 1980s also saw the rise of a subclass of rap called "gangsta rap." Its often profane lyrics glamorize gang-related subjects like violence and drugs. Another characteristic of gangsta rap is that it demeans women.

Despite these changes, some rappers still feature elements of black nationalism. Sociologist Algernon Austin writes, "Many of the leading rappers of the late 1980s and early 1990s used black nationalist themes and images in their work. As Jeffrey Louis Decker observed, black nationalist rappers drew their inspiration 'primarily from the black power movements of the 1960s and the Afrocentric notion that the original site of African-American cultural heritage is ancient Egypt.'"[35] (Afrocentrism is the argument that black Americans are culturally tied to Africa, particularly to the ancient civilizations of Egypt and Nubia.)

Some hip-hop nationalists wear clothing or jewelry that mimics black power activists such as Huey Newton. Chuck D, the leader of Public Enemy, once posed for a photo for *Spin* magazine that was almost identical to one taken of Newton. The rapper KRS-One did a similar restaging, emulating a famous photo of Malcolm X. Chuck D and his DJ, Terminator X, often wear

Early rap artists like Public Enemy, pictured, promoted black nationalism with their music.

medallions in the shape of the African continent, with colors that came from a flag designed by Marcus Garvey.

In addition to themes about black life in America, rap lyrics, particularly those by Ice Cube and Public Enemy, voice explicit support for black nationalist organizations (like the Nation of Islam) and their leaders. African Americans who take rap and hip-hop themes to heart feel a sense of racial pride and cultural identity that is the core of black nationalism. Another common theme of rap songs is criticism of white cultural styles, white politicians, and particularly white police, echoing yet another theme of black nationalism—separation from white society.

Graffiti

Graffiti is a public art form, a way to express one's identity, political affiliations, or social opinions. For hip-hoppers, it provides a way to comment on life in inner-city America. Graffiti artists scratch, draw, or paint words and images on walls, trains, monuments, sidewalks, and streets. When done without permission of the property owner, it is a crime—vandalism. When done with the owner's permission, it can be advertising and is sometimes considered fine art.

This form of public art or comment has existed since ancient times. Graffiti can be found on the historic buildings of Rome and Pompeii, as well as inside the pyramids of Giza in Egypt. The graffiti of the hip-hop culture first appeared in New York City in the 1970s. Inner-city blacks and Puerto Ricans started marking public places with "tags." The tags were large graphic letters and numbers that identified the "tagger," the one who drew the graphic. The first identified tagger was a Greek American artist who identified himself as Taki 183.

Another tagger was Tracy 168. Later identified as Michael Tracy, the graffiti artist became well known for his tags spray-painted on commuter trains. Speaking about his work he said, "My paintings are alive, strong and very bright. The color combos make it. After the colors, the challenge became who could do the biggest piece."[36] Taggers expanded their public markings to include slogans. These slogans were often comments on inner-city life or messages of encouragement for those who lived there.

Early graffiti served both as a competition and as a method of expression. It often reflected a rage against a society that did not pay attention to the children of the inner city. Graffiti became a way of gaining attention and becoming known outside of the artists' ethnic community. It also served as a public challenge of mostly white police departments and city governments.

Tags and slogans were not the only graffiti found in public places. Street artists known as "grafs" created large paintings on commuter trains and walls. Tracy 168 felt he had no competition in tagging, so he moved on to become a graf artist. Some of his wall paintings were business advertising, for which he was paid. The work he did for free was often a memorial to a victim of urban violence.

Tracy 168 was not the only graffiti artist paid for his work. Jean-Michel Basquiat, a graffiti artist working in the 1980s, became recognized in the world of fine art. His work has been exhibited and sold in art galleries in New York and elsewhere. Basquiat, however, has never turned away from the hip-hop culture that inspired his art. His work explores everything from African American colonial life experience to the street violence of

Graffiti artist Jean-Michel Basquiat gained fame in the world of fine art without compromising his themes of black nationalism.

modern inner cities. His black nationalist thinking—themes reflecting a desire to promote black unity, black pride, and to express frustration at the injustices he has observed—is clearly on display in his paintings.

The Future of Black Nationalism

Hip-hop art and music have brought economic power and social influence to the generation born between 1964 and 1984. Though hip-hop popular culture is found among youth of all races and in many countries, it is found primarily in the African American and Latino communities of the United States.

The young people of the civil rights era demanded fair treatment under the law and helped bring about legal changes to meet that demand. Now, a generation later, black youth are again beginning to make their views known to society at large. Sociologists have, for some time, wondered if the youth of the hip-hop generation would use their power and influence for political change. Two recent events—protests against budget cuts made by New York City's mayor and the candidacy of Barack Obama for president of the United States—have demonstrated that they will.

In the spring of 2002, hip-hop artists joined teachers to protest New York City mayor Michael Bloomberg's cuts in the city's education budget. Since participation in a protest movement requires organization, the Hip-Hop Summit Action Network (HSAN) was formed. The mission statement of HSAN reflects black nationalist thinking. Its history mirrors the actions taken during earlier periods that brought black people together to fight injustice. The organization was formed after a June 2001 conference organized by Russell Simmons in New York City. This youth conference was the first National Hip-Hop Summit, and its theme was "Taking Back Responsibility." Simmons created HSAN to fulfill the commitments made at that conference.

Hip-hop summits continue to be held. Like the black conventions of the mid-1800s, these meetings give attendees a chance to voice their concerns and to plan for future action to address those concerns. HSAN provides support for those who wish to organize communities into action for social change, just as the NAACP, CORE, and SNCC did during the civil rights era. It remains to be seen whether or not the activism of HSAN will have as much

Russell Simmons, chairman of the Hip-Hop Summit Action Network, at a youth voter registration event in Boston.

impact on race relations in the United States as the organizations of the Civil Rights Movement did.

Simmons and his organization launched a cross-country voter registration push in 2008 to encourage the hip-hop generation to vote in the primaries and general election. The hip-hop generation now has the numbers and the organization to bring social and political change to the country. The presence and popularity of a mainstream African American candidate for president of the United States—Barack Obama—helped spur this activism. Obama, though not running on a black nationalist platform, nevertheless elicited a great deal of black pride, optimism, and activism among many young black Americans.

Hip-Hop Summit Action Network

———■———

Russell Simmons, an artist manager, businessman, and philanthropist who is probably best known for his HBO series *Def Comedy Jam* and *Def Poetry Jam*, founded the Hip-Hop Summit Action Network (HSAN) in 2001 to provide money and other aid to people and/or organizations that need it. HSAN helps direct the energies found in the hip-hop culture into a positive force to give youth a voice in social issues of the day.

The organization believes the hip-hop generation can be a major force for change to help address the war on poverty and injustice. Its primary aim is to engage the hip-hopper in issues related to equal access to public education and literacy, freedom of speech, voter education, economic advancement, and youth leadership development.

Thanks, in part to the political activism of organizations like HSAN and other grassroots efforts, Barack Obama won the hard-fought presidential race on November 4, 2008, becoming the first African American president of the United States. Emotions ran high across the nation and around the world when the announcement of his election came. Many who were interviewed later said that they had not believed it possible for American voters to so overwhelmingly select an African American. They were also hopeful that such a landmark event would help usher in a new era of racial understanding in the United States. In four earlier historic periods African Americans banded together to demand social and political change in the United States. Black nationalism developed during the first of these periods and became a major part of the political thinking and action of black activists and others who sought equal treatment under the law during the next three. Will the hip-hop generation turn their version of black nationalism—black pride, racial solidarity, and economic self-determination—into action and create a fifth historic period of social and political change? Barack Obama's election seems to indicate that it may have already begun. However, the ultimate answer to that question and the future of black nationalism remains to be seen. It is now in their hands.

Notes

Chapter One: What Is Black Nationalism?

1. Quoted in Melba J. Duncan, *The Complete Idiot's Guide to African American History*. Indianapolis: Alpha Books, 2003, pp. 23–24.

Chapter Two: Beginnings of Black Nationalism

2. Quoted in John Bracey Jr., August Meier, and Elliott Rudwick, eds., *Black Nationalism in America*. Indianapolis: Bobbs-Merrill, 1970, p. 10.
3. Quoted in ushistory.org, "Mother Bethel A.M.E. Church." www.us history. org/tour/tour_bethel.htm.
4. James Forten, letter to Paul Cuffe, in *Africans in America: America's Journey Through Slavery*, PBS, 1998. www.pbs.org/wgbh/aia/part 3/3h484t.html.
5. Quoted in Wilson Jeremiah Moses, ed., *Classical Black Nationalism: From the American Revolution to Marcus Garvey*. New York: New York University Press, 1996, p. 6.
6. Quoted in Herbert Aptheker, *A Documentary History of the Negro People in the United States*. New York: Citadel, 1951, p. 155.
7. Quoted in Moses, *Classical Black Nationalism*, p. 16.

8. Quoted in Moses, *Classical Black Nationalism*, p. 139.
9. Quoted in Dean E. Robinson, *Black Nationalism in American Politics and Thought*. Cambridge, UK: Cambridge University Press, 2001, p. 18.
10. Quoted in Aptheker, *A Documentary History of the Negro People in the United States*, p. 365.
11. Quoted in William L. Van Deburg, ed., *Modern Black Nationalism: From Marcus Garvey to Louis Farrakhan*. New York: New York University Press, 1997, p. 10.

Chapter Three: From Reconstruction to the Civil Rights Movement

12. Quoted in Milton Meltzer, ed., *The Black Americans: A History in Their Own Words 1619-1983*. New York: HarperCollins, 1964, pp. 137–38.
13. Quoted in Meltzer, *The Black Americans*, pp. 150–53.
14. Quoted in Bob Blaisdell, ed., *Selected Writings and Speeches of Marcus Garvey*. New York: Dover, 2004, p. 3.
15. Quoted in Columbus Salley, *The Black 100: A Ranking of the Most Influential African-Americans, Past*

and Present. New York: Citadel, 1993, p. 80.

16. Quoted in Salley, *The Black 100,* p. 80.

17. Quoted in Bracey, Meier, and Rudwick, *Black Nationalism in America,* p. 191.

18. Quoted in Bracey, Meier, and Rudwick, *Black Nationalism in America,* p. 194.

19. Quoted in Bracey, Meier, and Rudwick, *Black Nationalism in America,* p. 192.

20. Quoted in Bracey, Meier, and Rudwick, *Black Nationalism in America,* p. 192.

21. Quoted in Bracey, Meier, and Rudwick, *Black Nationalism in America,* p. 199.

22. Quoted in Blaisdell, *Selected Writings and Speeches of Marcus Garvey,* p. 182.

Chapter Four: The Civil Rights Era

23. Quoted in *Encyclopaedia Britannica, The Annals of America, Volume 17: 1950–1960: Cold War in the Nuclear Age.* Chicago: Encyclopaedia Britannica, 1976, pp. 256–57.

24. Quoted in Robert Torricelli and Andrew Carroll, eds., *In Our Own Words: Extraordinary Speeches of the American Century.* New York: Kodansha America, 1999, p. 236.

25. Quoted in Torricelli and Carroll, *In Our Own Words,* p. 262.

26. Quoted in Kenneth B. Clark, *The Negro Protest: James Baldwin, Malcolm X, and Martin Luther King Talk with Kenneth B. Clark.* Boston: Beacon, 1963, pp. 25–26.

27. Quoted in Clayborne Carson, David J. Garrow, Gerald Gill, Vincent Harding, and Darlene Clark Hine, eds., *The Eyes on the Prize Civil Rights Reader: Documents, Speeches, and Firsthand Accounts from the Black Freedom Struggle, 1954–1990.* New York: Penguin, 1991, p. 252.

28. Quoted in Melba J. Duncan, *The Complete Idiot's Guide to African American History.* Indianapolis: Alpha Books, 2003, p. 205.

29. Quoted in Answers Corp. Contents: Biographies, "Stokely Carmichael," Answers.com, 2006. www.answers.com/topic/stokely-carmichael.

30. Kathleen Cleaver, interview, "The Two Nations of Black America," *Frontline,* PBS, spring 1997. www.pbs.org/wgbh/pages/frontline/shows/race/interviews/kcleaver.html.

31. Quoted in Algernon Austin, *Achieving Blackness: Race, Black Nationalism, and Afrocentrism in the Twentieth Century.* New York: New York University Press, 2006, p. 83.

Chapter Five : Black Nationalism and Popular Culture

32. Quoted in Austin, *Achieving Blackness,* p. 80.

33. Quoted in Austin, *Achieving Blackness,* pp. 152–53.

34. Quoted in Jeff Chang, "It's a Hip-hop World," *Foreign Policy*, no. 163, November/December 2007, pp. 58–65.

35. Quoted in Austin, *Achieving Blackness*, pp. 157–58.

36. Quoted in Bronx Mall, "Graffiti Wall Art by Michael Tracy." www.bronxmall.com/tracy168/past.html.

For More Information

Books

Susan Altman, *Extraordinary African-Americans from Colonial to Contemporary Times*. New York: Childrens Press, 2002. Collection of biographies of important but seldom-covered blacks in American history.

Editors of Time-Life Books, *African Americans: Voices of Triumph: Perseverance*. Alexandria, VA: Time-Life Books, 1993. History of blacks, beginning with African life to slaves to freedom to the present day. Lots of great pictures.

Sheila Jackson Hardy and Stephen Hardy, *Extraordinary People of the Civil Rights Movement*. New York: Childrens Press, 2007. Presents biographies of civil rights leaders who are not often covered in books about the period. Includes information on events leading up to protests.

Brenda Haugen, *Marcus Garvey: Black Nationalism Crusader and Entrepreneur*. Mankato, MN: Compass Point, 2008. Covers the life of Marcus Garvey.

Allison Lassieur, *The Underground Railroad: An Interactive History Adventure*. Mankato, MN: Capstone, 2008. Told from the viewpoint of a slave, a slave catcher, and an abolitionist.

Michael Martin, *Harriet Tubman and the Underground Railroad*. Mankato, MN: Capstone, 2005. History of the Underground Railroad in graphic novel format.

Diane McWhorter, *A Dream of Freedom: The Civil Rights Movement from 1954–1968*. New York: Scholastic, 2004. A look at the most turbulent years of the Civil Rights Movement.

Web Sites

Academy of Achievement: Rosa Parks Biography (www.achievement.org/autodoc/page/par0bio-1). Short biography with pictures.

African Cultural Center: Slaves (www.africanculturalcenter.org/4_5slavery.html). Text and large map showing the triangle slave trade routes and cargoes.

SNCC 1960–1966: SNCC and Black Power (www.ibiblio.org/sncc/black_power.html). Text and pictures.

Thurgood Marshall: American Revolutionary
(www.thurgoodmarshall.com/home.htm). Home page introduces the book written by Juan Williams. Site includes photo gallery, speeches, articles, and interviews related to Marshall.

Tuskegee Institute National Historic Site: Virtual Exhibit
(www. nps.gov/tuin/). Interactive tour of this national historic site.

Index

National Association of Colored People
  (NAACP), 39, 51
National Negro Congress, 49, 50
Nationalism, 10
Negro Emigration Convention (1854),
  29
The Negro World (newspaper), 41, 44
Newspapers, black, 26–27
Newton, Huey P., 64
Niagara movement, 37, 39
  leaders of, *38*
Nichols, Nichelle, *72, 73*
North Star (black newspaper), 27

O
Obama, Barack, 84, *85*–86
Ottley, Roi, 42

P
Parks, Rosa, 54, *55*
Plessy v. Ferguson (1896), 50–51
Powell, Adam Clayton, 67
Public Enemy, 80, 81, *81*, 82

R
Randolph, A. Philip, 49, *49*, 50
Rap, 78, 80
  gangsta, 80
  themes of, 82
Roosevelt, Franklin D., 50
Roots (TV program), 74
Royal African Company, 12
Russwurm, John B., 26–27

S
Schwerner, Michael, 59
Seale, Bobby, 64

Selma (AL), violence in, *59*
Sierra Leone Colony (West Africa),
  21–22
Simmons, Russell, *85, 86*
Slavery, 8, 11–13
Slaves, *11, 20*
The Souls of Black Folks (Du Bois), 37
Southern Christian Leadership
  Conference (SCLC), 56
Student Nonviolent Coordinating
  Committee (SNCC), 63

T
Television, 72, 74, 76–77
Terminator X, 81–82
Thirteenth Amendment, 13
Tracy, Michael (Tracy 168), *82, 83*
Tracy 168 (Michael Tracy), *82, 83*
Triangle slave trade, 12
Tuskegee Institute, 34, 35, 36
Tyson, Cicely, *74*

U
Underground railroad, 9, 20
United States, 11–15
Universal Negro Improvement
  Association (UNIA), 9, 40
Up from Slavery (Washington), 40
U.S. Constitution, 9
  post-Civil War amendments to, 13–14
  slavery codified in, 13

W
Walker, David, 25–26
Warren, Earl, 51, 53
Washington, Booker T., 25, 32, 36, 40
  black nationalism of, 34

Picture Credits

Cover, © Bettman/Corbis
AP Images, 55, 58, 59, 62, 65, 76
© Bettmann/Corbis, 33, 39, 46
© Corbis, 28
© Julio Donoso/Corbis Sygma, 83
David Corio/Michael Ochs Archives/Getty Images, 79
Hulton Archive/Getty Images, 45
Kean Collection/Getty Images, 11, 18
Michael Ochs Archives/Getty Images, 81
William Plowman/Getty Images, 85
Rex Hardy, Jr./Time Life Pictures/Getty Images, 49
Carl Iwasaki/Time Life Pictures/Getty Images, 52–53
The Granger Collection, New York. Reproduced by permission, 26
© 2008/Jupiterimages, 70
Library of Congress, 14, 20, 23, 25, 35
The Kobal Collection/The Picture Desk, 75
Paramount Television/The Kobal Collection/The Picture Desk, 73
Schomburg Center for Research in Black Culture, The New York Public
    Library, Astor, Lennox and Tilden Foundations, 38

About the Author

Charles George is the author of dozens of children's and young adult nonfiction books on a wide variety of subjects, including books on various world religions, ancient civilizations, American Indians, the civil rights movement, and the Holocaust. He taught history, Spanish, and math for sixteen years in Texas secondary schools before "retiring" to write full time. Charles and his wife Linda have together written close to sixty books. They live in a small town in West Texas.